RIDE THE WILD WIND

RIDE THE WILD WIND

C. WILLIAM HARRISON

CUTTING EDGE

ISBN-13: 978-1-954840-15-7

Published by
Cutting Edge Books
PO Box 8212
Calabasas, CA 91372
www.cuttingedgebooks.com

CHAPTER ONE

THEY FOUND HIM in a saloon on a raw and muddy side street off Front Street. He had hauled his table and chair back into a corner of the room, and was sitting with his shoulders wedged against the crotch formed by the two walls. It was the position a man would take when plagued by his conscience or pestered by implacable enemies.

It was also the position that a friendless man would take when he drank alone and gazed at the world around him with bitter defiance and rebellious challenge.

When they came into the saloon and saw him there he had a bottle of French wine clamped in one big hand, and was using it to beat out the thumping rhythm of a Yankee war song. *John Brown's body lies a-moulderin'* ... But his voice, alcoholically husky and somewhat off-key as he chanted those fiery words, was unmistakably that of a man from the rebel South.

At first Elise Casamore found it all but impossible to attach this gaunt, bearded man to the memory she had kept locked inside her all these years. This man seemed taller. Thinner, too. Too much length to fit her memory, and too many hard, sharp angles. And yet ...

She frowned uncertainly. "Are ... are you sure?"

"It's McCabe, all right," Lee Malvern answered.

Travis Hooker's grin was a thin mixture of amusement and dry malice. "Happens on the average of two or three times a season, according to what I've heard. He has hired on as everything

1

from pilot to roustabout, but he never lasts more than one trip up the river."

The hour was late, and the saloon was filled with weary silence and the sourness of raw whisky. The barkeep was watching them with a look of jaded indifference on his heavy, pallid face, a thin cowlick of jet-black hair combed severely across the balding dome of his head. Across the room a pair of boat hands, all grins and fawning chuckles, were cadging drinks from a drunken trooper, and making plans to roll him at their first opportunity. This side-street saloon was that kind of a place, the hangout of small-time grifters and thugs and derelicts, too down in their luck to give a damn.

In that dreary hush, Travis Hooker's voice was a dry, rasping sound as he chipped Elise's uncertainty away with gritty facts.

"Sooner or later, it always catches up with McCabe that he's a down-South man who went over to the North during the war. It takes more than a few short years to live down the Judas brand, and I reckon this fellow never will. Secceshers hate him for a turncoat, and most Yankees feel the same way. He's too stubborn to lie about it, or change his name. But he always manages to go on one whale of a bat after he's had the can tied to him."

The look of pity and shocked disbelief deepened in Elise Casamore's eyes. Could it be true that this bearded, hollow-eyed man was actually Branch McCabe? It seemed impossible. Not the Branch McCabe she remembered from all those good times before the war.

The light from the saloon's bracket lamps was not enough. Elise moved closer. No, it couldn't be him. And yet…

It was the shaggy, sun-bleached beard that gave him the rowdy look, and made a stranger of him. Beneath that, though, she detected the unforgettable pattern of bold cheekbones and wide mouth and the long slant of the jaw. Not a handsome face, but one—and Elise the girl sent this impression across the years to Elise the woman—one that a sculptor might have carved from strong stone, rough-hewn, and with the marks of chisel and mallet adding their own brash artistry. And now Elise could see the small Y-shaped scar he had received above the temple that day when he had pulled her out of the run-away surrey on her father's plantation.

Yes, it was Branch. This gaunt-faced man with the bottle in one hand and the walls of a fly-trap saloon at his back was the Branch McCabe she had once loved, then learned to detest.

The saloon owner came around the end of the bar, a look of uneasiness in his pale, watery eyes. He cleared his throat and tried to speak in the most amiable of tones.

"This here fellow a friend of yours, is he?"

Travis Hooker glanced around, his grin losing some of its saline humor. "We know him."

The saloonman kept worrying the bar-rag between his hands. His gaze drifted uncertainly to Lee Malvern, to the girl, then back again to Travis Hooker. It was not an easy matter for the owner of a saloon to bring up when he made his living by catering to river men.

"I don't want to sound unseemly," he said.

Travis Hooker waited.

The saloonman cleared his throat again. "I wouldn't want it said around that a man ain't welcome in my place after he has spent all his money."

Travis Hooker made no comment.

"What I mean is, it's getting late." The saloon owner shifted his shoulders uncomfortably. He blinked, then smiled apologetically. "It's after midnight, and... well, I guess you understand what I'm trying to get at."

"Not any," Travis Hooker answered shortly.

"What I'm trying to say is—no offense intended—I'd like to close up." The saloonman drew a slow, sighing breath. "Like I said, no offense meant, but... well, I'd consider it a favor if you'd take your friend out so I can close up for the night."

The mocking mirth edged back into Travis Hooker's flat-lipped mouth. Devils of derision were laughing in his pale eyes.

"This is your place of business, mister. You want this fellow out, why don't you just throw him out? It makes no never-mind to us if he collects a few lumps."

The saloon owner's eyes went wide and round. "Me? Me chuck him out—big as he is?"

"You're packing a lot of heft."

"There's a difference. Believe me, friend, there's a world of difference."

Travis Hooker laughed sardonically.

The saloon owner went on. "This one never gets drunk enough. You've never seen him like I have, I guess. Two weeks ago he wrecked Charley Halsom's place when they tried to heave him out. Last year it was the Palace and Ben Zwicker's place that made the mistake. Nobody hustles this big fellow out until he's ready to leave."

Travis Hooker looked around at the man at the table. McCabe seemed only hazily aware of their presence, and not in the least disturbed. Hooker laughed again, softly.

"So if you folks don't mind, late as it is … "

"We'll take him out," Hooker said.

The saloonman measured Lee Malvern and Travis Hooker with thoughtful skepticism. "You two? Just you two?" Then he groaned wearily. "Oh, Lordy!"

Branch McCabe had stopped chanting the song about John Brown's body. He tilted the bottle to his lips and drained it. He wrapped his big hand around the neck of the bottle, and shoved up out of his chair.

He was unsteady on his feet. He was a tall man, towering, and there was a hint of cheerful challenge in the way he stood there with his big shoulders backed up against the corner of the room. He didn't say anything. He didn't know exactly what was coming off, but in the soggy haze of his mind there were shadowy memories of other times like this, in other saloons where he had looked into bottles for oblivion. And he stood there, waiting.

Travis Hooker spoke shallowly. "Let's go, McCabe."

"Ain't ready to leave yet."

"You've had enough for one night. Let's get going, man."

Branch McCabe blinked owlishly across the table at the two men. "D'I know you?"

"No," Travis Hooker answered.

McCabe's grin was slow and wide, with the brine of the condemned in it. "Seems like I'm always beating hell out of strangers. Strangers are always beating hell out of me, seems like. Only two of you this time, though. Only two. Not half enough to handle it, boys."

"Branch, Branch!" Elise Casamore whispered in a soft, aching way.

"Not half 'nough," McCabe repeated, wagging his head.

The derision danced higher in Travis Hooker's pale gaze, and his laughter was a thin and shallow sound lacing the room's smoky hush.

"You're not seeing straight, jocko. The owner of this flea-trap is here with us. Makes three, by my count. More than enough, I'd say."

McCabe pondered this information. He gazed at each of the three men before him solemnly, then shook his head again reprovingly.

"Still short one man," he said, his words slow and thick. "Usually takes four. At least four, gen'lemen."

Travis Hooker snorted softly, and reached out and skidded the table and chair aside, out of his way. McCabe tottered, then steadied his balance. He lifted the bottle in his big hand, and stood waiting. There was no anger in his face, only stubborn challenge and a kind of deep and weary fatalism.

"C'mon, c'mon," he muttered, and stood braced for their attack.

Travis Hooker was a man with a strong appetite for this sort of thing. He had handled these big fellows before, and he had never yet met one too tough to be handled. There were ways and means that Hooker had learned from practice and experience, and now he motioned Lee Malvern and the saloon owner further apart from him to divide McCabe's attention and split his defense.

This maneuver did not bother Branch McCabe any; such strategy had been used on him at other times in the past, with varying degrees of success. It didn't matter now any more than it had mattered to him before.

The saloon owner got his bung-starter from behind the bar, and took a firm grip on it. He asked nervously, "We gonna rush him? Is that the ticket?"

"It's your joint," Hooker said, and his laughter was a malign, jeering sound. "You go at him first, why don't you, and then me and Malvern will start climbing him."

The saloonman rolled his eyes. "Oh, no!"

"He's only one man."

"You never saw what he done to Ben Zwicker's bouncers last year."

"He's drunk as a bat."

"Not drunk enough, he ain't. Friend, I've learned a thing or two about this fellow … "

"Ah, hell!" Hooker grunted contemptuously, and temper skidded all patience out of him. He went drifting toward the man in the corner with the smooth, balanced movements of a pacing cat.

Travis Hooker had a talent for this sort of thing. When McCabe rocked forward and struck at him, he let the clubbing bottle miss him by the narrowest of margins. He spoke with soft and brittle savagery to the two men flanking him.

"Next time I draw him out," he addressed the saloon owner, "you clout him one with that bung-starter." And then to Lee

Malvern: "If he doesn't drop, you make a pass at him from your side. This big ox is made to order for what I can hand him once you crack him open."

Hooker started drifting forward again, but the girl caught at his arm, holding him back.

"Not that way," she cried out. "Please … I don't want him hurt."

"It won't hurt at all," Hooker told her thinly, and the malice in his eyes was a bright and brittle mockery. "Once I get this big fellow set up, he'll never know what hit him."

"Please don't," Elise said again. "Let—let me try first."

She stepped up to Hooker's side, then a little past him. Against the dimness of the room her face was quite pale, and thudding through her mind and her heart was the love of the girl she had once been and the loathing of the woman she was now. She tried to tell herself that it did not matter how much the man confronting her was hurt. Yet, she knew it did matter.

He seemed to tower in the corner of the room, at bay and defiant. A bracket lamp burning at one side cast the shadow of a hawk's wing across his face, drawing into sharp relief the haggard lines and the hollows beneath his eyes.

He, Elise told herself, had made his foolish decision, and had been hammered down and defeated by it Men of the South hated him, and men of the North distrusted him. Contempt had followed him everywhere along the river since the war, brutally marking him. And now he was a derelict, a jackstraw, a common drunk.

No, she did not want him hurt, not if it could be avoided. As she gazed up at him, she realized grimly that the love of Elise, the girl, was dead, and now the loathing of Elise, the woman, was gone. What this man was and what he had become no longer mattered to her.

From this moment on, Branch McCabe's place in her world would be accepted with hard and frigid indifference. He was bone and muscle, and had a mind that understood the dangers

7

of the Upper Missouri. She needed those qualities to help her carry out this grim and dangerous thing she had set herself to do. On Branch McCabe could depend success or miserable failure. She needed his strength and his skills, and she would use him as she would use a tool, coldly, calmly, emotionlessly. And with the cleverness that only a woman possessed.

She cried out to him in a voice made soft and sad to fit the demands of her deception.

"Branch, Branch! Don't you recognize me? Don't you remember me at all?"

She saw him sway his head back and forth, as though trying to clear his vision. Not much light reached into this far corner of the room.

"It's me, Branch—it's Elise!"

He drew a slow, sighing breath. "Who?"

"Elise, Branch—Elise Casamore."

He seemed to stop breathing.

"I'm right here in front of you. You're looking at me, Branch. Don't you remember me at all?"

Deep back in Branch McCabe's eyes the shadows of a dim memory were moving uneasily. But when a man had drunk as much as he had, he couldn't trust the sound of a voice, even a girl's. He couldn't trust his own eyes. After a week on two-bit whiskey and French wine, a man's mind could play savage tricks on him, making him hear voices where there was only silence and see images in places where there was nothing at all. It had happened to him before.

"I'm here, Branch—right here in front of you. Elise Casamore—surely you haven't forgotten me!"

He could see only the slim contours of the girl's body, the blurred oval of her face. A never-forgotten face. He knuckled his eyes with his left hand. It didn't help any. He blinked at her.

" 'lise?"

"Yes, Branch."

"Mus' be another trick … another damn trick."

"No, Branch. I'm real. I'm here."

He had to be sure. No matter what those three men had in mind for him, he had to know for sure about this Elise-image blurring before his eyes. He rocked forward, squinting at her.

" 'lise Casamore?"

"Yes, Branch."

He took a slow, groping stride toward her, so that he might see her better. Was it real, or another tormenting dream of the past? If only he could touch her …

He rocked forward another step. He reached his hand out toward her.

He had the vague impression that he must have been struck from behind by one of the men. But he wasn't aware of any pain or the thudding impact of a blow.

He took that one slack-kneed stride toward the image of the girl, and then his legs caved under him and he fell, out cold.

CHAPTER TWO

H E CAME AWAKE SLOWLY, by degrees. At first he heard the sound of a steamboat's whistle. It seemed muffled and far away, sounding off at regular intervals the way a packet often did when it was measuring echoes as it groped through dense fog for the levee.

And then he heard voices, a girl's voice and then a man's.

The girl's first. "He's starting to come out of it, I think."

"It's about time. What did this fellow try to do, drink St. Joe dry? He's been under for close to thirty hours now."

"Give him some more coffee, Mr. Yandell."

"He's a'ready sloshing like a water-heavy keelboat."

"Some more coffee, Mr. Yandell," the girl said.

McCabe was conscious of a pair of calloused hands gripping his bare shoulders, boosting him up into a sitting position. He didn't think he felt like sitting up, not yet; he grunted irritably, tried to shove the man's hands off him, and received a mild clout on the side of his jaw for his trouble.

"Drink this," the voice of the man said, the patience of Job in it.

The coffee was hot and strong. It burned its way down Branch McCabe's throat, and hit his stomach like the wallop of a fist, jolting him fully awake. He coughed, choking, and blinked his eyes open in the brilliance of sunlight streaming through an open window close above his head.

For a moment he was blind and confused, his mind still dulled by his long bout with the bottle. Then he forced his eyes open again, squinting against the sunlight. He was on a bed and a man was bending over him. He couldn't recall ever seeing the man before. But he detected a twist of wry sympathy in the fellow's tone of voice.

"I won't even ask how you're feeling."

McCabe groaned softly. "Lordy!"

"Know just what you mean," the man commented dryly, and mirth rustled deep in his throat. "I've been there a few times myself, and the torments of hell could be no worse. In case you're curious, my name is Clee Yandell."

"Yandell...?"

"I've made a few records in saloons down at Natchez-under-the-Hill that would crowd the one you made in St. Joe. You want some more coffee?"

"Just let me die," said McCabe.

"Mister, it wasn't my idea to wake you up to your miseries," Clee Yandell answered meagerly. "When a man in your condition is being dragged back to his torments, you can generally count on a woman being behind it."

"A woman...?"

Branch McCabe turned his head. And then he saw her. She was standing at the foot of the bed, watching him soberly. Recognition was swift and sudden; it was like a blade twisting inside him, bringing back all the hurts he had tried so long to forget.

"It's been a long time, Branch," he heard her say.

He didn't answer. Here was the girl he had gone to school with in those long-ago days before the war. Here was the girl he had sat with in church, and afterwards walked beside along dusty plantation roads.

Those had been times when he had been not quite a man yet, nor she a woman. The awkward years when a boy-man and a girl-woman become frighteningly aware of maleness and femaleness, and of hungers rising powerfully between them—the rich, lingering years before the war had swept them apart with its floodtide of madness and malice.

"Elise…"

He searched her eyes, but saw only a cool remoteness and the chipped edges of unforgotten rancors. He was conscious of the changes the years had brought to her. The shy wonderment and leggy adolescence were gone from her now.

She was a woman now, with a woman's rounded symmetry and a mature beauty in the lines of her face. Gazing at her, Branch McCabe was reminded of how much he had given up that day when he had ridden out of the South to join the Federals in a hard and brutal war that had ripped friends and neighbors apart with its unrelenting savagery.

The thought was a bitter and painful one to Branch McCabe, but he had no regrets. A man did what he had to do. A man had to shape his life according to his own creed of right and wrong, or he was nothing. No matter how close he had once been to Elise Casamore, she would never get an apology from him. Nor would he ever expect one from her.

Clee Yandell grunted. "How about some more coffee?"

McCabe shook his head. The man's tone of voice had changed. McCabe looked at him. The expression strengthening in Clee Yandell's eyes and around his mouth was a familiar one. Yandell was remembering everything he had ever heard about this Branch McCabe—a man who had gone over to the North in a war against his own people. The look of malice and cold contempt had haunted Branch McCabe relentlessly; it was always the same.

"I've been forgetting some things about this fellow," Yandell commented sourly, and set the cup of coffee down on the floor. "You don't mind, Miss Casamore, I'd like to get some fresh air. It's kind of foul in here, you know what I mean."

Clee Yandell was gone.

"Was a time not long ago when I would have cracked that fellow's jaw for what he said."

Elise's tone was dry, remote. "You should be accustomed to it by now, I should think."

McCabe shook his head. He smiled wryly. "It was taking too much of my time. Too many jaws to be cracked, Elise, without ever changing any opinions about me."

He became conscious of a gentle rolling motion beneath him. He looked around, realizing for the first time where he was. He was in the cabin of a river packet. Outside, he could hear the gusty chugging of engines and the heavy, rhythmic sloshing of the boat's bucket-planks at the stern. He raised his eyes. Through the open window and swung between the craft's high stacks, he could see in reverse lettering the name of the boat. It was the *Southern Belle*.

The pain of the sudden memory that came rushing into him must have showed in his eyes, for there was accusation and a thin edge of malice in what Elise Casamore said to him.

"Yes, Branch. It is quite a shock, I imagine, to find yourself on the same rebel packet that you helped sink during the war." Her smile was thin and frozen with condemnation. "You were on the Federal gunboat that sent the *Belle* down, I've been told. It was the *Lexington*, wasn't it?"

McCabe nodded. He didn't say anything. He closed his eyes, and the echoes of that violent night on the river were in him once again, thudding against his conscience.

Yes, Elise, I was there. Of all men, it had to be me. We'd spent most of the night chasing a packet that was trying to slip up the Arkansas river with munitions for Quantrill's guerrillas. Along toward dawn we cornered the rebel boat in a shallows. It turned out to be your daddy's boat—the Southern Belle. *I prayed to God they'd surrender without a fight, but they refused. They started their run to break past us, and then our 64-pounders opened up....*

And later he had heard gossip in riverfront towns that the packet had been refloated after the war and put into service again. But the bodies of the dead and dying could never be repaired and given new life. He looked at the girl, and asked the question that had haunted him since that night of violent battle.

"Your father and brother—were they on board when the *Belle* went down?"

There was acid in Elise's steady gaze. "What's the matter, Branch—is your conscience bothering you?"

She knew how to cut a man. "I want to know, Elise."

She looked at him for a while longer, in stony silence. Then she shook her head. "This boat was only an investment. My father wasn't a riverman. Neither was Phil. They—they were both killed at Yellow Tavern."

"I'm sorry, Elise."

"It's too late for that, don't you think?"

Her malice was quiet and cold, refusing to accept any pity from him. He looked away. She would never know the torments he had carried in him since that fight in the shallows of the Arkansas.

He brought his gaze back to her. Against the mahogany paneling of the cabin's door, she stood slim and very straight, a girl who was pretty but who could never be called beautiful.

There were small imperfections—the faint scattering of freckles across her nose, the sassy tomboy tilt of her chin, the somewhat overly-wide mouth that hinted an inner warmth and generosity that were no longer to be seen in her eyes.

A man saw these small defects but instantly forgot them, his fancies carried away into an illusion of faultless loveliness by the striking contrasts of her coloring—rich black hair and golden skin and eyes of an incredible blue-green that in actuality were neither color.

It wasn't forgiveness that had made her hunt him down and bring him here; that much was at once obvious to Branch McCabe as he studied her.

He spoke quietly. "What is this all about, Elise?"

Her reply was crisp, cool, remote. "You were out of a job and the *Belle* needs a captain who knows the upper Missouri. That's all there is to it."

McCabe smiled dryly. As simple and uncomplicated as that. Nothing personal. The past they had once shared was gone, dead. This was a business deal, nothing more. She had to have a pilot for her boat, and she had sought out the only one available, a drunken, haunted man who had sat in a fly-trap saloon thumping out the beat of the bitterest of all war songs with an empty wine bottle clenched in one big fist.

She was offering him nothing more than a job and that was all right with him. He would not beg. He had his own stubborn pride. He could be to her as she was to him, cool and impersonal, a stranger.

He searched back through his foggy memory of the night before. "I seem to recall two or three men in the saloon with you. There was something said about them hauling me out of the place, which means there was probably a fight."

"There was no fight."

He looked down at his hands. No marks of a brawl on them. He smiled sourly. "I must be slipping. Usually there are some heads cracked, my own included, in the process of chucking me out of a saloon."

"And you're proud of that record?"

"Not particularly."

"Nor ashamed of it either, I suppose."

He shrugged his big shoulders.

"No fight at all," Elise said in a thin, stinging way. "You passed out like a common drunk."

"I've probably done it before."

She was being carried away by emotions she had fought hard to control. "You have that sort of reputation, it appears," she told him icily. "Branch McCabe, the turncoat! McCabe, the saloon-buster! Ever since the end of the war, you've been trying to find something in bottles. What is it, I'd like to know—your self respect?"

McCabe watched her wearily. He did not reply.

"Your self respect, Branch McCabe, or escape from your conscience?"

He sat quietly in the bed, the blanket pulled high around his body. He had been hurt before, and knew he would be hurt again. It was part of the price he had to pay. He had learned to carry his hurts deep inside him, and when they became unbearable, he drowned them with the contents of a bottle. For the price of a bottle, he could find a few blessed hours of oblivion.

He looked at Elise without resentment or anger. "Is this why you hauled me out of that saloon and sobered me up—to rawhide me because I didn't believe in what the South was fighting for?"

Her silence was as cutting as her voice had been, and he felt his own temper begin to pile up.

He said thinly, bitterly, "You've waited a long time for this chance, haven't you? All right, Elise, you've used your whip and spurs. You've said everything you kept stored up to tell me. Now if you will kindly get out of here I'll put on my clothes and go my own way. I don't need a job bad enough to work on this packet."

She didn't move. She stood there staring at him, the echoes of her brittle spite standing in her eyes.

McCabe was conscious of his nudity beneath the single blanket. His clothes were across the room, on a chair. He brought his gaze angrily back to the girl.

"Are you going to leave, or do I have to get dressed in front of you?" he demanded.

Nothing changed in her face. McCabe's temper crowded higher and higher.

"All right, then!" he grunted savagely.

He wrapped the blanket around his body, and got out of the bed. He was a tall man, towering, with wrath in the hard planes of his face. He pulled the blanket tight around his middle, tucked a corner of it under to hold it in place. He turned, and started across the room toward his clothes.

A sudden impulse halted him. He swung sharply around and went to the girl. He towered over her in a way that made him acutely conscious of his male height and her feminine smallness, but through all this rode the hard heat of his resentment and rankled anger.

He didn't say anything. He gripped her shoulders with his big hands and pulled her to him, close to him. He saw startled alarm rush hot and furious into her eyes. But that didn't stop him. He locked his left arm tight around her, and with his right tilted her face upward to meet his own.

She struck at him with her fists as he kissed her. He raised his head briefly, laughing softly and mockingly as he stared down at her. He felt the stinging flames of her nails raking his bare chest as he locked her against him and kissed her a second time.

Then all at once his wrath fell apart, and a sense of shame and overpowering regret swept through him. Anger was no excuse for what he had done. The way he had kissed her had been brutal, almost contemptuous. He had been wrong, all wrong.

It was all mixed up inside him—the memory of picnics and lawn parties at the plantations their parents had owned in Louisiana, of laughter shared in those lazy, carefree times before the war, the hunger and loneliness of all these years since the war—hurt and defiance and angry retaliation. It was for all these reasons that he had acted so impulsively, but not any single one alone.

"I'm sorry, Elise."

Looking down at her, he could see the pallor of her cheeks and the bruised redness of her lips. She was, he thought, on the verge of crying.

"I'm sorry," he said again.

The cabin door swung open, and Travis Hooker came into the room, a lank, angular man with tawny eyes and smoothly sculptured features. Hooker halted shortly just inside the door, a wary alertness taking hold of him.

"Anything wrong here?"

McCabe left it for Elise to answer. Her crew would be swift to punish an insult, hard-fisted ex-rebels who would find satisfaction in laying the whip to a man like Branch McCabe.

"No," Elise said. "Nothing wrong, Travis."

Hooker shrugged, and gave his full attention to McCabe after that. He measured McCabe's height and heft as though searching for a weakness and secretly finding it.

"You'll take the pilot's job, I reckon."

Here was a man, Branch McCabe thought, who was sharp and hard and knowing. It irritated him to feel that he had been measured so swiftly and accurately, and he let a note of curtness rear up in his short reply.

"Depends."

"So? On what?"

Elise was watching.

McCabe spoke bluntly. "I'm fed up with having my part in the war thrown in my face. I did what I thought was right, and there were a few thousand other Southerners who felt the same way. The war is finished and done. As long as I am on this boat, I want it left that way."

There was derision in Travis Hooker's tawny eyes. "A mighty big order for a man of your reputation. It won't be easy to sell to the Johnny Rebs we've got in our crew."

"Those who won't buy it, I'll know how to handle. It wasn't the crew I was thinking about."

Hooker shrugged, watching Elise narrowly and making no comment.

McCabe looked at the girl. Her eyes and face had changed. She tried to smile. He searched her eyes for the old rancors and prejudices of a lost rebel cause, but he could no longer see them. A woman, he thought, knew all the many tricks of pretense and deception. A man could never be sure. Yet her smile and what she said seemed sincere and genuine.

"I've tried to hate you, Branch, but I was wrong. I realize that now. Branch … I want us to be friends again."

Real, or a woman's clever duplicity? He had no way of knowing. A man could only accept what he saw and what he was told when he dealt with a girl like Elise Casamore.

"You've got yourself a pilot," he told her, and knew that only time could prove whether he had allowed himself to be deceived.

Travis Hooker and the girl were gone. McCabe dressed and went out on the packet's promenade. A nagging restlessness was in him as he stood at the railing and watched the muddy currents of the river slide past below.

Bit by bit, small shards of gossip and rumors that he had heard about the *Southern Belle* were filtering back to him. About the boat and its hard-fisted crew. About the roustabouts who had been recruited from the dives and deadfalls of riverfront towns from Natchez-under-the-Hill to St. Louis.

Ex-rebels and unrepentant renegades, according to the gossip he had heard along the levees. Rowdies and high-rollers, many of whom had blooded their guns while riding with Charley Quantrill's band of cut-throat raiders.

A troubled throught stirred in Branch McCabe's mind. Legends had been woven around this packet he was on. On a night of violent battle, the *Southern Belle* had been smashed and sent to the bottom. But she had been raised and refloated again. She was strong again, manned by a crew that had never forgotten the ringing defiance of the rebel yell.

What place did Elise Casamore have in this boat and its tough crew? The question skidded deep into Branch McCabe's mind, nagging him. But there was no answer.

CHAPTER THREE

THERE WAS NOTHING in Branch McCabe's constitution that made it easy for him to tolerate chicanery. He was a big blunt man whose nature it was to walk into a problem head-on, to batter it down and chuck it aside or be defeated by it. It went against his grain to play a subtle game, and it rankled even more to feel that he was being slyly used by others.

He had no delusions about Elise Casamore. She was a girl of indomitable will and unbending principles. The obvious fact that those principles had been shaped and tempered by old traditions and prejudices of the rebel South added to McCabe's uneasiness.

More than anything else, he wanted Elise's friendship. She represented a deep and treasured echo of a good and less troubled time in his life. No man could ever seal himself away from the memories and dreams of his youth. They were in him, a part of him and they never died, McCabe had learned in a score of riverfront saloons where the oblivion he had searched for in bottles had been brief and bitter and utterly futile.

He wanted Elise's friendship, but he knew he did not have it. Each day as he pushed the *Southern Belle* northward into Indian country against the roiling currents of the Missouri that fact settled deeper and more undeniably in his mind.

She was smiling and casual on the rare occasions when they were together, but always he detected the chill of unforgotten rancor in her. It was something that he sensed, but could never see.

A man he could have crowded into a corner, and cracked open with plain words and hard knuckles. But not Elise. She possessed skills and devices that no man, however adroit in the ways of women, could cope with. McCabe stumbled and groped through a maze of doubts and misgivings, but always she remained smiling and benign and completely inscrutable.

In the end, he was forced to accept the situation between them at its surface value. It was a truce, and nothing more than that. She had needed a pilot for her boat, and he was the only one available familiar with the hard and deadly currents of the upper Missouri.

She had needed a pilot, and he had accepted the job. Why she had hired on this tough crew and gang of roustabouts, McCabe could not understand. Perhaps it was because she had put too much trust in Travis Hooker. A hard one, that fellow. A shrewd and scheming man. He would, McCabe thought, bear much watching.

At Omaha, they nosed in at the levee to pick up several crates of rifles and small-arms ammunition that had been freighted overland to this remote landing, consigned to Colonel Maxwell Cady's Eleventh Cavalry, at Fort Abraham Lincoln. Captain John Myles and a company of rookie troopers under Lieutenant Stacey Pryor came aboard, and the packet shoved out into the heavy currents once again. Ten days later, just below the Diablo Narrows, a sudden storm came roaring out of the north, and forced McCabe to tie in at the bank for the night.

At six o'clock next morning the storm was gone, the last low gun-metal clouds breaking apart under fitful gusts of wind. The air was damp and raw; winter had been slow to let go this year, and in sheltered places the earth was still hard with frost.

From where McCabe stood in the pilot house of the *Belle*, he could look down at the bloated currents of the river. Even with the full tide of the spring flood past now, the Missouri was a ponderous thing. He could feel the power of it bucking and thumping the hull of the boat, and see the wrath of it in the endless debris floating past—deadwood and full trees aborted from a thousand places up-river.

Raising his eyes, he studied the mouth of the Narrows less than a quarter of a mile upstream. There were those on board—Captain John Myles included—who swore it was impossible for any steamboat to be pushed through the brawling currents and cross-tides of that Narrows. But today Branch McCabe knew it would be done. It had to be done. The dangers of the river were far less to be feared than a Sioux war party catching the packet tied in at the bank, a sitting target for their bullets and arrows.

McCabe turned and stepped out of the pilot house, a big man who was already feeling the pressures of the new day. As he went down the stairs, he saw the girl at the forward railing of the hurricane deck. Immediate displeasure broke loose in his eyes. For Elise to stand there after dark was one thing. But for her to be there in this graying light was entirely another matter. The light was good enough now for accurate shooting. He had repeatedly warned her. Sioux hostiles were without conscience when they were painted for war and looking down the sights of a rifle.

The thought was a fearful one, and he swung his gaze sharply to the hills above. Nothing moved. Nothing threatened. This gave him only meager relief, for this was May in the year 1871, and only the foolish or innocent could feel secure along this wild stretch of the Missouri.

Yet if there was any immediate danger from Indian hostiles, the two scouts Captain Myles had sent out into the hills last night would have sounded a warning by now. And Elise was not entirely alone and unguarded. There was that young pup of a lieutenant—Stacey Pryor—squatting behind the sheet-iron parapet on the leeward side of the deck. McCabe snorted sourly. *Full of gallantry and heroics, that young squirt. Chances are he wouldn't recognize an Indian if he saw one.*

McCabe moved his shoulders irritably, and started across the rain-washed deck toward the girl. He was tall, with weight to his shoulders and a reserve in the lines of his face that bordered on taciturnity. Weather had darkened him, making his eyes appear startlingly bleached in contrast. He carried himself with the easy balance of a hunter, and the look of a hunter was in his eyes, the hard patience and restless energies held under stern control.

Elise jerked sharply around as he came up behind her, alarm clenching in her face. She tried to cover this sudden fright with a quick smile that touched stinging heat to McCabe's vexation. It was this sort of foolish bravado, he had long ago learned, that filled so many graves along this stretch of the river.

"How many times do I have to warn you, Elise? The way you were standing here! What if I'd been a Sioux? I'd have had a knife in your back and your scalp ripped off without you ever knowing what killed you."

He used his voice roughly on her, trying to drive the picture of Sioux cunning and brutality into her mind.

"I was restless, Branch. I couldn't sleep. I wasn't thinking, I guess. I won't do it again. I promise."

She was too compliant, too contrite, too damned conciliatory. McCabe stared at her in baffled, impotent exasperation, wondering what it would take to open the secret doors that she was keeping locked against him.

"There's something else we've got to get settled," he told her crossly. "It's about the hardcase crew you've got working for you."

"What about my crew?"

"I don't like the looks of them."

Her eyes were guarded, unreadable. Rain glistened in her hair. "This is a rough country, Branch. I was advised that I would need a tough crew."

"But not the kind you've got on board," McCabe answered flatly. "I've been up this river on all kinds of boats, but I've never seen a crew the likes of yours. Renegades and rebel die-hards, all of them. Quantrill men. Malvern, Yandell, and Travis Hooker used to ride with that cutthroat, I've heard it said."

"Do you always believe everything you hear?" Elise asked coldly.

"I've had a few days to look over your prize collection of hardcases."

The girl smiled up at him thinly. "Charley Quantrill and his men must have given you a hard time during the war for you to be nursing so much hate against them."

"I haven't forgotten a town named Lawrence. Women raped. Children murdered."

"That was war, Branch."

"Not the kind of war decent men fight. Not the kind of war your daddy and brother fought."

A wet wind came out of the hills in a gusty rush, the sudden down-draft sending smoke boiling around them from the packet's high stacks. The air cleared. Anger was in the girl's eyes, hot and furious.

McCabe spoke meagerly. "You and your crew live in different worlds. You're up here, and they stay down below. You ought to go down there once in a while and get better acquainted with your men."

She was outraged by the thought. "The main deck is no place for a woman. You ought to know that."

"You stopped being a woman the day you decided to go into a man's business. Come along with me, Elise, and see for yourself what kind of men you've got on your payroll."

He took her arm, and they went down the stairs. Below, the deck hands and roustabouts were hard at their chores, pausing as McCabe and Elise went past to follow the girl with bold speculation in their eyes. Each grinning man added heat to McCabe's temper, but he was in no mood to do battle against what they were so obviously thinking. He kept a lid clamped down solidly on his wrath.

A red-necked roustabout said something in a low voice, and a burst of laughter, loud and ribald, sprang from the remark. McCabe saw color rush into Elise's face, but he said nothing. If she did not know already, it was time for her to get it straight in her mind what breed of men she had working for her.

They were tough, hard-bitten—all of them. Renegades and outcasts. Rebel die-hards, with the rancor of the war still festering in them. Their malice did not take much to trigger. McCabe remembered the swift swirling violence of Lee Malvern's roustabouts when they ganged up on a pair of rookie troopers who had blundered in their way a week ago. And that Ohio bluecoat, staggering drunk after a night's bout in the packet's saloon, had not gone over the deck railing by accident. This was the hard and gritty temper of the crew that McCabe wanted Elise to know about.

As they walked, he gave mind to the ship's rigging and gear. The spars were in place, ready for use should the *Belle* hit a sandbar. He paused at the bow to examine the ropes that lashed down the crates of rifles and ammunition destined for Fort Abe Lincoln and Cady's Eleventh. The ropes had loosened since yesterday's inspection. He ordered Lee Malvern to have additional lashings put around the crates.

The marks of many brawls were on Lee Malvern's weathered features, and forty years on the river had not sweetened his soul. A squat, vinegary man with arms and shoulders all out of proportion to his height, he reared back on his heels and stared at McCabe with a truculence he made no effort to conceal.

"I know a thing or two about boating that maybe you didn't learn while you were shooting rebel packets out of the river for the Federals. Nothing short of a tornado could knock these crates loose."

"Then see that they're tied down for a tornado," McCabe told the man stiffly.

It was the wrong tone of voice to use on Lee Malvern, and swift temper came boiling up into his eyes.

"Sure, sure," he shot back savagely. "I'd just never get over it if you or any of your bluecoat friends happened to get hurt by these crates busting loose."

McCabe touched Elise's arm, feeling the hot challenge of Malvern's eyes on him as they turned away.

A tough crew. A crew to be feared. Quantrill men. Hotheads who had earned their spurs with Mosby and Jo Shelby. Rebels who had been the pride of Beauregard, Forrest, Cleburn and Bragg, veterans of Shiloh, Yellow Tavern, Five Forks and Dinwiddle Courthouse. Violence had honed and hardened them, and in their veins flowed the unforgiving malice of men who had cursed Lee at Appomattox and returned to the river with weapons in their hand and hate in their heart.

McCabe paused, turning to Elise. "You want to hear more?"

There was stubbornness around the girl's mouth. "What Malvern said was only talk. Nothing but talk, Branch. He didn't really mean what he said."

McCabe moved his shoulders irritably. Nothing he could say would convince her. Perhaps, he thought bitterly, there was nothing he could show her that would convince her. The pride of the Casamores was in her, and all the old loyalties and prejudices.

They moved on. They came to the engine room. McCabe had his look inside at the giant Negro who, stripped to the waist, was chucking wood into the open firebox. The heat of this place struck McCabe like the blow of a fist, as he saw by the steam gauge that the *Belle* had for several minutes now been ready to cast off.

"Ease off a while, Jubal. You build up any more steam, and those boilers are going to let go."

The Negro butted the iron door shut with the heel of his hand. Turning, his grin was slow and wide as he mopped his glistening shoulders with a stained rag.

"That's what I been thinkin', Cap'n McCabe," he said, and laughter rumbled in his deep chest. "We set a keg of nails on that there safety valve, and we can make ourselves some good Yankees out of them bluecoat troopers up above."

McCabe spoke carefully. "Now who ever put that idea in your head, Jubal?"

"Why, nobody in pa'ticular, Cap'n. It's what most of the roustabouts and crew talk about doin', one way or 'nother. You're a Southrun man, ain't you?"

"You know I am."

"Then I reckon you feel the same way about Yankees as the rest of us."

Branch McCabe's smile was slow and meager. "You surprise me, Jubal. I can't get used to the idea of you wanting to kill men who helped set you free."

"Free? Now that is purely strange, Cap'n. When I was a owned man I used to get good food, enough clothes to wear and a house for me and my woman. I could hear her singing, and see my young'uns playing around the house when I came out'n the fields. 'Pears to me a man ain't got need for any more than that."

McCabe said nothing.

"Then Old Abe, he up and said, "Jubal, you're a free man." Only I don't rightly know what free is, Cap'n. I still eat the same victuals, and wear the same kind of clothes. But I cain't be with my woman at night now, and my young'uns a'most don't know me any more, seldom as I see them. I never had to work so hard back in Louis'ana before I got 'mancipated."

It was, McCabe thought, the voice of a man lost and lonely in a world suddenly too large for him to comprehend. "You're getting cash money for your work now," he said.

"Yassah," Jubal answered, and nodded slowly. "Is that what being free means? Is that all it means, Cap'n—cash money jingling in a man's pockets?"

McCabe looked at the girl beside him. He said nothing.

Jubal made a vague motion with his huge hand. "I reckon that's why I keep thinkin' about clompin' down the safety valve with a keg of nails. Blow up enough Yankees, and maybe I could get myself un'mancipated again, Cap'n. What good is being free if a man cain't be home with his woman and young'uns?"

Clee Yandell, the engineer, was at his levers, impatient to get the packet's wheels turning.

"How much longer?" he demanded crossly. "We could have moved out half an hour ago."

"Can't leave until those two scouts of Myles' get back," McCabe answered.

Yandell's grin was malevolent. "They're already back. Got back five minutes ago. You ask me, things are going to warm up mighty fast on this boat, once we hit that Narrows. Myles and that slick-eared lieutenant of his'n are already starting to sweat. Their scouts brought news that a Sioux war party will be waiting on the bluffs when we go through the Narrows."

Then Yandell's malice took on a more brittle shine. "Get the picture, McCabe? You in that glass pilot house, and Yankees catching hell on the decks. I hear tell the Sioux are getting hold of guns these days."

"You're forgetting one thing, Clee."

"So?"

"They'll be shooting at you, too."

Clee Yandell was a short, blocky man with eyes like the rounded ends of bullets. He snorted dryly. "I've been shot at before, McCabe. But it's you and the bluecoats who will be the main targets when the Sioux cut loose on this packet."

McCabe touched Elise's arm, and they turned back along the deck. First Lee Malvern, and then the giant Negro, Jubal. And now Clee Yandell had made plain his malice against Yankee troopers.

They were not alone. There were others among the crew like those three—die-hard rebels who were tough, seasoned, unrelenting. Men of proud Southern stock who carried their hurts on the surface, raw and unhealed. Appomattox had been the surrender of armies, but not of the scattered hold-outs who even now still raided and plundered the border country.

These men of the *Belle*'s crew were of the same bitter breed as Lane, Shelby, and Quantrill, dedicated to the same implacable war of retaliation and the hope of fanning into life the flames of a new rebellion. In all these men lived the same furies, savage and unyielding, riding the harsh winds of reckoning.

McCabe paused at the deck stairs. Beside his towering height, Elise seemed tiny, almost fragile. Yet in her was more strength and courage than he had ever found in any other girl.

"Well, Elise?"

"It's talk. Nothing but talk."

"I wish I could believe that."

Some of the fine color had drained out of her face, but her gaze was steady on him, defiant.

"Anywhere you go in the South, you can hear the same kind of talk. I could say the same things, and ... and mean every word."

"You don't really mean that, Elise."

Her eyes were hard, angry. "Every word—every damned word, Branch McCabe. I'll never forget what the North did to my family. My father and brother killed. Our cattle driven away to feed Yankee troopers. I saw them take our grain, and loot our cellar. My mother went hungry because of Yankee troopers and carpetbaggers. I'll never forgive them for that."

"Or ever stop hating them?"

"Never!"

"Hate is an ugly thing, Elise."

She laughed thinly, scornfully. It was a shocking thing to hear. It sent a coldness like a wintry wind rushing through him. He stared at the girl. She had Elise's body, Elise's eyes and nose and mouth. But this wasn't the Elise he had carried in his memory. She was someone else, a stranger. Someone he had never seen before.

She broke the silence between them, her voice hard, brittle. "Suppose it were true that my men are hoping to stir up a new rebellion. What would you do about it?"

"Try to stop them."

"They wouldn't let a man like you stand in their way. They'd kill you."

"Maybe."

"And knowing that, you'd still try?"

"Yes."

"I wouldn't," Elise said, her voice cold, flat, obdurate. "I think I would even help them."

"You're building a wall between us, Elise."

"The same wall you built the day you left the South to join the Yankees. It's your wall, Branch McCabe, not mine."

"I'm sorry, Elise."

"So now you know how I feel," she said stonily.

"So now I know, Elise."

She started to swing angrily away from him, then halted the movement abruptly, and turned back. She gazed up at him with eyes that were stubborn, wintry, then little by little he saw the anger drop out of her face and a small, wry smile come to her lips.

"I think we're a little premature in going to war against each other, don't you think?" she said then.

McCabe waited.

Her voice when she spoke again was quiet, controlled. "This little battle we've had, Branch—it was based on nothing more than your impressions of my crew. But you're wrong—I know you're wrong."

"I hope I am."

She made a small distracted gesture with one hand. "I didn't mean what I said about helping starting a new rebellion—I didn't really mean that, Branch."

"I know you didn't."

"There's been too much hurting and killing and dying."

"Four years too much, Elise."

"But that doesn't change how I feel about the North. I want you to know that."

He waited.

"I guess you have a right to know why I brought the *Belle* up this river," she told him. "I watched Yankees empty our barn, drive off our livestock, burn our fields. I watched them loot our home, smash our furniture, set fire to our house. No reason—no reason at all. The war was over when it happened. But they did it, and I'm going to make them pay. I intend to use this boat to collect all the debts the North owes me. I will haul freight for Yankees, but they are going to pay every red cent I can gouge out of them. Do you understand what I'm saying, Branch?"

There was a grimness in her eyes, a hard and cold determination. "I'll be smiling and nice to them all, but they are going to pay to the limit for the services of my boat. They owe me that much, and I intend to collect in full. That is my reason—my only reason, Branch—for coming up this river."

Elise was gone, McCabe stood at the foot of the stairs, the echoes of what the girl had told him still rolling through his mind.

He was a man of hard and realistic principles, and four years on a Federal gunboat had given him his fill of war. Right or wrong, the South had made its fight and been defeated. This was the time for forgetting, for healing old wounds. But if Elise wanted to be implacable in her dealings with Yankee traders, he couldn't blame her. For her to gouge them to the limit was no different nor worse than the profiteering being done by carpetbaggers along the southern stretches of the river.

Her crew, though, was a far different matter. Those men had never stopped hating. The war still flamed in them. The thought that settled in McCabe's mind was like chipped ice. *They've heard about the campaign to be made against the Sioux. They came up here to make all the trouble they could for General Sevier and Cady's Eleventh.*

He was a man balanced on a saber's honed edge. To put the troopers on their guard would bring into focus again all the old hates and suspicions. The rumors would spread from officers to men; violence would flare between Yankee hotheads and the *Belle*'s hardcase crew, and the Sioux would be waiting along the banks to massacre the survivors.

Too late now to turn back. He had to push on, to yank the fuse out of this powder keg, or be destroyed by it.

Once in a Louisiana bayou settlement he had seen a man dying from tainted food. That day a Creole woman had come into the camp and forced the dying man to eat more and more of the tainted food, until the stomach had rebelled at last and emptied itself. Purged, the man had recovered.

There were times, Branch McCabe knew, when poison could be its own cure.

He was only one man. A man alone. What he had in mind could, he knew bleakly, put him in a sudden grave, hated by rebels and Yankees alike. And hated also by Elise.

CHAPTER FOUR

E STOOD ALONE in the pilot house, watching through the open windows as the roustabouts came trudging up the stairs to the hurricane deck, each man lugging a bulging sack of grain across his shoulder. At Lieutenant Pryor's directions, the bags were deposited on the deck to form crude battlements behind which troopers could crouch when the fighting began.

McCabe studied Stacey Pryor with critical interest. The man was young, lean as saddle leather, and had cleanly-chiseled features. He was the kind of officer, Branch reflected, that hard-bitten troopers would heartily resent at first contact. But there was nothing brash or overbearing about this young lieutenant. He was green and uncured and feeling the same harsh pressures that were in all others on the boat; but he wasn't letting them rattle him.

A good head on his shoulders, McCabe thought; his first fight, and scared as hell that he won't measure up.

The last sack of grain was dropped into place. Pryor studied the pattern and potential of this crude bastion, then stepped back to where the two scouts, Charley Lowe and the Indian, Curly, were standing.

McCabe watched as Pryor spoke to Lowe. Lowe turned, a weathered, bone-lean man who was wearing a cut-away hunter's coat that bore the stains of many camps. He appraised the contours of the wall of bagged grain, squinted up at the bluffs above the Narrows, then nodded his approval.

In McCabe's mind this thing, of all others, was the key to Stacey Pryor's worth. Those shoulder boards haven't made him too tony to ask advice.

This was a time when the pulse of the packet increased to a hard and heavy thudding in the hearts of all men. The women and children had been sent to the safety of their cabins. Arms and ammunition were issued to every trooper, crewman and male passenger as Captain Myles gave his final orders for the fight that was coming.

Shifting his gaze, McCabe saw Travis Hooker watching these preparations for battle with sardonic eyes. The Mississippian was lank and loose-coupled, with the scar of a Yankee sniper's bullet furrowing one dark cheek.

Hooker smiled sardonically up to the window of the pilot house, and it was as though the man had spoken audibly to McCabe. *Take plenty of time going through the Narrows. With bluebellies for targets, I want to furnish the Sioux with some mighty fine shooting today.*

And across that distance, Travis Hooker's malign gaze carved a second felon image into McCabe's mind. *This is why we came up here—to put Yankee troopers in their graves. You try to buck us, mister, and we'll put you in yours.*

A sudden weight seemed to come down on McCabe, huge and terrible. Malvern, Clee Yandell, the giant Negro, Jubal; Sam Carthage, whose wife had been ravaged and left to die during the war by a drunken Yankee deserter, and Travis Hooker, whose face bore the scar of a sniper's bullet—the brute malice of all these men was like a noose drawing tight and hard around him. There was no escape. He was captain of the *Southern Belle,* but he was nothing. Get in their way, and they would stomp him under. There were enough of them to do it. They had killed before, and were willing to kill again. And if Elise tried to stop them... That thought, stark and terrible, was like chipped ice spilling through McCabe's mind.

He dug tobacco out of his pocket, and filled his pipe. His hands were not steady.

He stepped back from the window, back from Travis Hooker's feral gaze. He stood beside the packet's great spoked wheel, head down and staring at his hands—big strong hands that had once opened up the earth and sowed the seeds of growing things. Hands that had struck men in anger and manned the weapons of Federal gunboats through four brutal years of warfare.

But his hands were not steady now.

He scuffed a sulphur match into flame, and got his pipe going. It was the damnedest thing. No matter how hard he locked the muscles of his arms, he could not stop the trembling of his hands.

The door opened behind him. Turning, he saw Elise come into the small compartment. She halted, staring at him.

"Branch, what's wrong?"

He didn't answer.

"The way you look, the way you're shaking! Are you ill?"

"I'm scared, Elise."

"Branch, Branch!" she whispered.

"I can't help it, Elise. The crew and what they came up here to do. They don't care what happens to the women and children we've got on board. They're praying for the Sioux to attack. They're praying for Yankees to be killed, and they don't care what happens to the boat. It's like a mountain smashing down on me, Elise, and I can't get out from under. That's why I'm scared."

"I can't believe that," Elise said. She came around the huge, spoked wheel, came close to him. "You're wrong about them, Branch, all wrong."

He shook his head. Only a man could see and understand the rancor that blazed in those rebel die-hards. Only in men did hate run so deep and relentless.

The boat was ready, the time had come. Hap Burwell and Tully Kennerly were fore and aft on the main deck, axes in hand.

McCabe sent his signal down to the engineer, calling for power, and Clee Yandell rammed his levers home. The chugging of the engines took on a deeper tone, and the bucket-planks at the stern began threshing the river into muddy froth. The packet began moving. McCabe shouted below.

"Hap! Tully! Cut her loose!"

The axes glittered in swift arcs, severing the shore lines. Gripping the spokes, McCabe threw his weight against the wheel, hauling it over and around. It took the power of a strong man to maneuver a packet when the river was at flood. The bow of the *Southern Belle* nosed away from the bank, and was struck at once by the full impact of the swollen currents. She shuddered and steadied. McCabe rang for more steam.

He watched the riverbank slip away behind him and held the packet steady, reaching for deeper waters. He was aware of Elise's eyes on him, of the tension taking hold of her face. Those same hard pressures were also in him.

Out yonder, beyond the rounded bow, were the dangerous waters, roiled with their freight of debris; out there were the wild slashing currents where an undetected sawyer could rip the hull of a boat open and bring swift destruction. A man had to look close to avoid those dangers.

He had one brief look up from the river, up to the rim of the bluffs above the Narrows.

And he saw the Sioux warriors, stripped and painted, etched against the skyline—waiting.

CHAPTER FIVE

A<small>ND NOW THERE</small> could be no retreat.

Here where the river came churning out of the Narrows, the cutbanks of the bluff lifted raw and sheer, and along the high rim the hostiles watched and waited.

There had been no shooting—not yet. There were wise heads among those paint-daubed warriors who had schemed other attacks such as this one, and knew that the bend of the Narrows would give them their deadliest advantage. From that high thrust of land they could lay down a murderous fire on the decks of the packet as it fought the turbulence of the river.

Gripping the wheel, Branch McCabe held the packet to the main channel. Only by the gradual shifting of the banks could he measure the *Belle*'s progress, and he took each yard with worry and anxiety.

The Missouri at flood was a savage thing. Compressed by the sharply curving Narrows, it came rushing against the boat with a heaving, bludgeoning impact, pitching the bow violently. The shock of those pounding torrents telegraphed up through the hull and superstructure, and beat thumping pulses against McCabe's feet. Big as he was, there were times when the wheel was almost more than he could control.

A hundred worries tormented him. He shot a glance across his shoulder, and saw Elise rising to peer out one of the windows. He shouted harshly at her.

"Damn it, Elise, I told you to stay down!"

"They're only watching us, Branch."

"For God's sake, do as I say!"

She dropped back to the low bench, and a small breath of relief flowed through McCabe. Those heavy sheet-iron plates lining the lower walls of the pilot house offered a measure of safety, but there was no protection for the windows.

The Missouri was always an implacable enemy, and a man at the wheel could never relax his vigilance. A roustabout crouching at the bow of the main deck suddenly shouted and pointed short ahead. McCabe's hands went sweaty around the grips of the wheel. He spotted the sawyer that was all but hidden beneath the bloated dark currents of the river; he bucked his weight hard against the wheel, hauling the *Belle*'s nose away from the snag.

Danger was everything and everywhere. A man had good reason to hate the river at times like this.

The movement of the cutbanks had slowed until now they were almost stationary. McCabe rang for more steam, and felt a gulp of relief when he got it. How much more power he could get from Clee Yandell he had no way of knowing, for there was a strict and fatal limit to how much a man could demand from his engines.

The channel was starting its hairpin bend to the west now, turning the currents choppy with crosscuts and whirlpools. Under this growing stress, the pounding of the river against the hull magnified hugely until the reverberations were like those of a wagon jolting in the ruts of a road.

The window suddenly exploded in front of McCabe, and he heard Elise's brittle cry of alarm.

He shouted at her. "Stay low—stay down!"

Another bullet crashed close by, and from the deck below Captain Myles bellowed a command; the roar of gunfire shattered the day.

The mind of a man registers many images during the tight moments of battle—the keening of close bullets, the stinging stench of gunsmoke, the harshness of voices crying out in anger and agony. The racket swelled until it became a throbbing din that the hearing would not accept, and after that, the violence was a thing felt in the bones and sinews and the heart.

The windows of the pilot house were breaking apart under the murderous barrage being poured down from above. A bullet tore a splintered scar across a spoke of the wheel just above McCabe's hand, leaving a tingling numbness in his fingers.

From somewhere below a trooper's stricken cry lifted stark and terrible, then fell away. McCabe heard soft laugher close behind him. It was Travis Hooker. "There's one damned Yankee paid off."

McCabe released one hand from the wheel and smashed Hooker across the mouth, a savage blow.

"Damn you, Hooker! Grab up a rifle and start using it!"

A fury of pure hate flared up in the man's eyes, and against it McCabe cursed Travis Hooker bitterly.

"You blind, brainless fool!" And temper raised McCabe's voice to a full shout. "If those devils up there take this boat, you'll get the same treatment as the Yankees. Start using your gun, damn you! You've got your own hide to worry about now!"

The hate in Travis Hooker's eyes was a wild and wicked thing. He pawed his mouth with the back of his hand, violence flaring through his face. His rage that moment was capable of murder, and there was a gun under his belt. His hand stabbed down to it.

"No!" Elise cried out. "Please don't!"

Her voice cut through to the one small remnant of sanity left in him. It halted him rigidly. He turned his head slowly to look at the girl in a vague, hate-blinded way.

Elise's voice caught at him again. "Don't do it .... please. We wouldn't have a chance without a pilot ... "

It took time for her voice to work its way through Travis Hooker's blazing fury. After a while, he grunted. He moved his head back and forth, like a man trying to clear an overpowering obsession out of his mind. What the girl said made sense.

He was no fool. He could wait. His voice was hard, heavy, thick. "All right."

He hauled himself around and picked up a rifle from the rack. He looked at McCabe again, and now a smile was on his bruised lips, thin and biting.

"Later, fellow. I'm not finished with you, not yet."

He heeled around, and slashed shards of glass from the broken window with the barrel of his rifle. He fired, levered, and fired again. Powdersmoke began building up in the small room, black and acrid.

In Elise's eyes was a bitter reproach. *That was a mistake, Branch. He'll never forget what you did.*

The thought was as plain as that in Elise's eyes. And Branch McCabe didn't give a damn.

The packet inched on, bucking the rushing power of the river, slashed by gunfire and thudding arrows. The apex of the bend slipped past the bow with agonizing slowness, and the savagery of the Sioux was relentless.

On the high rim of that bluff a medicine man, all feathers and horns and garish paint, danced and howled and made his obscene gestures of challenge and taunting defiance. The young bucks blazed away with reckless ferocity, but there were wise heads among the warriors who held steady and fired deliberately. Trade rifles boomed, and arrows hissed downward; Spencers and big-bore Henrys, torn from the hands of Fetterman's slaughtered troopers not many months ago, raked the decks with inexorable fury. It was a murderous gauntlet for a riverboat to run, for there was no retreat in that twisting narrows and the hard, rushing currents of the river fought implacably against escape.

Men had fallen on the decks below. Through the racket of gunfire, McCabe could hear voices crying out in shock and agony. That he himself had not been hit was a thing he could neither comprehend nor give thought to. No time for fear. No time for prayer.

In a bleak and dogged wrath, he drove the boat on against the rowdy turbulence of the river, measuring his progress by the almost imperceptible movement of the cutbanks. That fallen sycamore he had used as a marker was behind him now. Another rod, and he would be abreast of that gray hump of granite thrusting out of the bluff's raw shoulder.

The packet seemed to be slacking off. He rang for more steam, but the little that Clee Yandell gave him was not enough. And all at once the malice of the *Belle*'s rebel crew came back to hit him, like a wintry wind roaring through his mind. *We'll give the Sioux plenty of time to do their killing.*

It was a stark and fearful thought. He yanked the signal cord again for more power, but he got none. The packet was no longer making any headway; she was barely holding her own against the rushing currents of the river.

He heard Elise's panicked cry. "We've stopped moving, Branch!"

From the edge of his vision, he saw Travis Hooker jerk around from his rifle, a sudden sickness of dread clenching in his face. A Sioux bullet struck the will close by the man, and went squalling away. Hooker ducked violently aside, and he yelled at McCabe, harshly.

"Damn you, get this boat out of here!"

McCabe flared back at him. "Maybe you can get something out of Yandell. I rang him twice without getting anything."

Hooker grabbed up the tube, and shouted down to Clee Yandell for more steam. But Yandell didn't have any more to give.

McCabe's gaze ran along the ragged line of the near bank, searching desperately. Nothing for him there. He swung his attention to the opposite bank, and saw an ancient cottonwood towering at the water's edge, a hundred feet ahead. There was no time for caution or careful reckoning. He heaved his weight against the wheel, fighting it over.

The packet's nose swung slowly and ponderously; it began lunging wildly as it took to the cross-currents. That moment the wheel was all that Branch McCabe could manage, bucking and back-lashing violently against him as the packet nosed deeper into the cross-cuts. There was a growing numbness in his arms and shoulders.

It was deadly water he was moving into. He was aware of that. Here the back-wash of the river swirled against raw cut-banks, and there were rocks and snags beneath those surging dark currents that could rip a hull open. There were signs for a knowing man to read, a gamble to be risked only by the foolish or the damned.

He worked the boat to within twenty feet of the bank, and could get no closer. And now there was a racket of movement and voices rising to him from the decks below through the tumult of gunfire from the Sioux on the opposite bank. Lee Malvern had fought other floods in his forty years on the river. He knew what had to be done.

Through the shattered window, McCabe saw a heavy rope uncoil through the air, reaching out from the bow toward the riverbank. Then he saw one of the crew go racing across the deck to hurl himself upward, leaping mightily for the shore. There was a sudden roar of gunshots from the Sioux. Mid-air, the man was struck by a violent impact. He hit the water, a redness following him under. He didn't come up again.

And now Lee Malvern himself was moving out to the edge of the deck to measure the distance; he backed away to make room for his run, a man too old for such things, but knowing it had to be done. It was like the keening defiance of a rebel yell ringing through Branch McCabe's mind as he watched.

Then another man was lunging past Lee Malvern to make that desperate leap toward the bank. Arching upward and outward from the deck, straining for distance across the roiling currents of the river, dropping now toward the water's edge. Scrambling up the bank, and grabbing up the heavy rope. Running toward the cottonwood while Sioux bullets slashed the earth around him.

It was Stacey Pryor, lieutenant of Cady's proud Eleventh.

Valor did not belong only to the gray of the South. This thought rose strong and glowing in Branch McCabe's mind, like a saber stabbing sharp and clean through the bitterness of his rebel crew.

On this day, valor belonged to a lieutenant who wore the blue of the Eleventh.

The line was fast around the cottonwood and the capstans were drawing the heavy rope in, breaking the grip of the river as it hauled the packet out of the Narrows. On the opposite bank, the gunfire of the Sioux was thinning out. McCabe eased in closer to the shore, and took Stacey Pryor aboard.

The *Southern Belle* had won her reprieve.

CHAPTER SIX

ALL THAT LONG DAY McCabe had fought the river as he would an enemy, and now at dusk he nosed the *Belle* against the lee banks of Squaw Island and watched two of Malvern's hands leap ashore to secure their lines.

It was a good place for a tie-in, a safe place. At this point the Missouri was comfortably wide, and the low rolling hills were well out of the range of Sioux rifles. Here a man could get out from under the pressures of the day, and ease the aches out of his body. McCabe couldn't remember when he had felt so thoroughly used up.

The fight at the Narrows was eleven hours and forty hard miles behind him, but its harsh echoes were still in him and the faces of the dead and dying would not let him alone.

He thought of the Indiana man whose body lay wrapped for burial. Seth Apperson was the name. Or maybe it was Appleton. He wasn't sure which, and he supposed it didn't matter much, not now. The man had been a cabin passenger bound up-river with his mind set on the free lands of Oregon. He hadn't been a fighter, but one of those quiet, gentle men who live close to the earth and its growing things. Now he was dead, another name to be added to the thousands before him who had left good homes to travel to their graves in a wild and lonely land.

As he stood at the railing of the hurricane deck, it was easier for Branch McCabe's mind to accept the deaths of the five men in blue. They had been troopers, paid to fight and bleed and die. But for the Indiana man he felt pity and weary regret, for his would be a grave that would be lost and unremembered after tomorrow.

From below, McCabe could hear the muted chanting of the roustabouts as they finished their day's chores. Fore and aft on the main deck, torches of pine knots were blazing in their steel baskets to hold back the deepening dusk. In another hour most of the crew would be settled down to their endless games of *vingt-et-un,* or chewing over again and again the events of the day. Somewhere across the far hills a prairie wolf yammered at the rising moon, then fell silent. Tomorrow will be a clear day, McCabe thought emptily.

He was aware of footsteps coming up from the cabin deck; turning, he recognized Travis Hooker's high-shouldered shape moving toward him through the darkness.

"I've been looking for you," the man said in his blunt, head-on way.

"You've found me," McCabe answered, and rummaged through his pockets for his pipe and tobacco.

He took his time loading the old briar and getting the smoke going, aware that where Travis Hooker went danger followed. Under the flame of the match, the flat planes of the man's face held no readable expression.

"I just came from the hospital room," Hooker stated. "In case you're interested, a trooper named Chesney died a few minutes ago."

McCabe drew a slow breath, making no comment.

"Six bluecoats dead, and another eight wounded. I'm curious what you've got to say about that."

McCabe said meagerly, "Get to the point, Hooker."

"I'll do just that, by God! I'll lay it on the line for you, and you'd better take pains to get it straight. Hauling this boat out of the Narrows this morning was one thing, but running away from that fight is something else. With half a chance, the Sioux could have crossed off twice as many bluecoats as they got."

There was temper rising in Branch McCabe, warm and bitter, but he held a lid clamped down on it. He spoke slowly. "And dead Yankees is what you want?"

"You know damn well what I want. You've been prying and pecking around. You know damn well what every man in the crew came up this river to get. But don't get the idea that what you've guessed and what I'm telling you will cut any ice. There's nothing you could do that would stop us."

"You're sure of that, are you?"

"I'll tell you something else, McCabe. Elise Casamore didn't hire a single man in the crew until after I'd passed on him first. I picked the ones I wanted for this boat, and booted off all the others. Does that mean anything to you?"

McCabe's pipe had suddenly gone rank and sour in his mouth. He knocked the ashes out of the briar, grinding them under his heel. "It's beginning to."

"I'll lay it out plainer," Hooker said in his harsh, head-on way. "You're captain and pilot of this boat, but you're only a name. You're the man at the wheel, but with my crew you're nobody. You're nothing."

McCabe breathed slowly, conscious of the bigness of his own body as he measured the man before him. Travis Hooker was lank and lean, and carried thirty pounds less weight. He looked easy enough to handle, and this, McCabe knew, could be a fatal deception. It was a grim conviction that crawled along his nerve ends, sending echoes of dire warning through the hollows of the mind.

Travis Hooker, he suddenly knew, was like no other man he had ever come up against—a man physically and mentally engineered to be precisely what he was, completely and thoroughly dangerous. No warmth, no impracticality, no vulnerable quirks. Here was one who could kill without passion or pity, whose violent savagery was rooted in the dark and terrible caverns of never-forgiving malevolence.

There was no swagger or bombast in what the man said; it was the hard-knuckled arrogance of complete surety and towering competence.

"You hear me, McCabe? On this boat you are nothing but a cardboard captain. You wear the white cap and make all the noises, but I am the one who pulls the strings. If it suits my purpose to take over the *Belle,* I can do it—any time."

His eyes were like the rounded ends of bullets. "It's me the crew comes to for the orders that count. Don't you ever forget that, mister. One word from me, and I can have you stomped down to size—or killed." His voice was one of contemptuous challenge and brittle ultimatum. "Do you think that's all talk?"

McCabe could feel his temper piling up in him in thick, hot waves, and against it he drew a slow, deep breath. There was a wicked little derringer under the man's belt, concealed by his coat. Hooker had used it before, and was willing to use it again. It was a thing to remember.

Hooker spoke dryly. "Maybe you need some help deciding," he said.

Then he moved, no word or expression to betray him. He moved with explosive abruptness. McCabe felt a sudden burst of agony deep beneath his ribs, without ever knowing where the blow had come from. Hooker threw his legs and hips and shoulders into a second smashing blow. It seemed to Branch McCabe that he had been sledged in the stomach by an ax.

An overpowering weakness swept through him, and he rocked forward, trying desperately to get his hands on the man, but he couldn't. He heard Hooker's whispery laugh of derision, and was jolted erect by the heel of the man's hand smacking solidly against the point of his jaw. Lights exploded behind his eyes.

Another blow came out of nowhere, driving deep into his middle. He heard the gusty whistling of wind rushing out of his lungs, and in a fury of frantic desperation he threw his fist at Hooker's face. He missed. He couldn't understand why. He knew what to do, but for some reason that he could not comprehend he was unable to do it. His muscles refused to obey.

Hooker came sliding in close, ripping short, shoulder-driven blows to the heart and stomach, each one jarring its own grunt of agonized protest out of McCabe. He pawed at Hooker, trying to shove him back and put an end to this brutal punishment that was tearing the last shards of strength out of him.

But he couldn't even touch the man. Travis Hooker was an elusive shadow that danced back from him, then came lunging in again with bleak and pitiless savagery. McCabe heaved a ponderous blow at the man, but he didn't hit anything. The momentum of that wasted effort toppled him forward to the deck on hands and knees.

He heard the man's snort of contempt as he crouched there, sick at the stomach and gagging for breath.

"You're a big one, McCabe. But size ain't enough. You'll never see the day when you can handle me, and don't you forget it."

McCabe's arms caved under him, and he felt the side of his face smack solidly against the deck. He groaned softly, and rose to his knees again.

"Not finished yet," he muttered thickly, the only thought in his mind to get up to his feet so he could have another try at his attacker.

"Not done yet, Hooker."

It was more than he could comprehend, that he had been handed so thorough a beating without landing a blow of his own. He had made a mistake somewhere along the line. Next time he would do better. He was big enough. He had the heft. No man had ever been able to smash him down and keep him there with fists alone.

He pushed the deck away from him, stolidly and stubbornly trying to get on his feet again. His sense of balance was a careening shambles. Rising, he felt the deck lurch out from under him, dropping him backwards heavily on his buttocks. A sense of deep and stinging shame swept through him, and he rolled over, cursing softly and savagely, and tried again. He made it this time.

He hauled himself around, pointed himself doggedly at Travis Hooker, and heaved himself at the man. But Hooker was no longer in front of him. Something hit the base of his neck, like the blade of an ax. He was halted by the pain that went shooting into his head. He grunted, pulled himself around, searching the darkness for Hooker. Something—someone—moved close in front of him. McCabe hammered at the man with both fists, and then felt himself spun around and slammed backwards violently against the wall of the pilot house. For the first time in his life, he tasted the sickness of utter defeat.

"So now you know," he heard Travis Hooker say flatly, contemptuously. The man's voice was a blade laying McCabe's shame wide open, and spilling salt into it. "Any time, mister. Any time you say I can give you the same, and more."

He leveled his finger at McCabe as he would a gun. "Now you listen close, fellow. It's no penny ante operation that brought me up here. I came up this river to put a knot in the North's tail that they'll never untie, and I was trained for the job by experts."

Hooker stood braced against the slight rolling of the packet, a man of tempered steel, without pity or charity.

"Don't get the idea I'm the only card in the deck. This is big—big. Frank and Jesse James and most of Quantrill's old outfit are itching to cut loose on the Yankees again. The Youngers have a bunch together and waiting. Marmaduke and Bill Gregg, too. And Jo Shelby with his Iron Brigade. We've got others like them lined up, from California to Georgia. From here on in, Appomattox is just a scrap of paper. The South is only starting to fight, and before I'm finished up here I'll have an army of Indians hacking at the Yankees this time."

McCabe stared numbly at the man. The Jameses and the Youngers. Gregg and his Border Ruffians, and Shelby's Iron Brigade. The bushwhackers who had ridden under the perverted

Quantrill—those men and others out of the same unrelenting mold. Another rebellion, another war in the making! The thought was a sickness spreading through him as Hooker's words beat into his brain.

"And don't ever get the notion that you or the Casamore girl can stop us. One word from either one of you to the bluecoats about us, and you're both dead. You hear me? I've got a charge of gunpowder fused up on this boat where you could never find it. You keep that in mind, mister. You get out of line just once, and I'll set off a blast that won't leave a whisper of this boat and every one on it."

McCabe breathed shallowly. He couldn't speak. The cramping agony that Hooker had sledged into his body was beginning to leave him. But the gagging sickness wouldn't let go.

"You want to come in with us, we can use you. Or it makes no never mind if you stay out. We're organized. We can get along without you. Only don't ever try to stop us. You get bucky just once, and we'll dig a grave for the girl alongside yours. You hear?"

"I hear you."

"One more thing," Hooker said, and his voice was like the slashing of a whip. "You laid a hand on me today. You ever do that again, McCabe, I'll gut-shoot you."

The man was gone. McCabe pushed himself away from the wall of the pilot house. It took an effort to straighten his body. He felt like he had been worked over with a mallet, each small movement bringing a tormented protest from the places where Hooker's blows had landed.

He handled me like I was nothing at all. The thought was an acrid one that damned him bitterly for his failure to land even one blow of his own. In the space of short seconds, he had been broken apart and smashed down in complete defeat. The fact was almost more than he could get fixed into his mind.

He was a big man, a towering man who had fought his share of brawls and known a few defeats. But this time he had been

handled like a spoiled brat, and to admit that was the most stinging humiliation of all.

Maybe I was too sure of myself. Next time I'll be ready for him.

But he knew suddenly and dismally that there could never be
a next time. Travis Hooker's warning had been plain, unmistakable. As final as the bullet from a gun, as inevitable as death itself.
*He'd do what he said. He'd murder Elise and every passenger on
this boat.*

Branch McCabe realized bleakly and bitterly that he was no
longer his own man.

For this hour on, he belonged to Travis Hooker.

CHAPTER SEVEN

Going across the deck toward the stairs, Travis Hooker's gaze, always prowling on the alert, picked up Elise Casamore standing tense and motionless at the after-railing of the hurricane.

A quick heat of nettled anger ran through him that he had failed to notice her there when he came up the stairs in search of McCabe. But it did not matter; no harm done. Instead, he decided shrewdly that it was all to his advantage that she had witnessed the easy efficiency with which he had smashed down the captain of her boat. From now on she would realize there was a better man on board than Branch McCabe, and out of this knowledge would rise a fear that would keep her humble.

But when Hooker's restless gaze picked up the head and shoulders of the Yankee trooper rooted in startled immobility halfway up the stairs, his temper took on a hard and dangerous edge. It was obvious that this man had also witnessed his brief but brutal brawl with McCabe. The alarm etched in the trooper's face was easy enough to read. *He saw too much; he heard too much.*

The thought ran roughshod through Travis Hooker's mind, raw with urgency. He went past the girl, ignoring her. Elise he could deal with later, but this Yankee could not wait. As he reached the head of the stairs, the trooper came alive, shocked out of his stunned rigidity. He heeled sharply around, starting toward the deck below. Hooker spoke amiably.

"Anything I can do for you, friend?"

The trooper halted, gazing upward across his shoulder. He was small and compact, with skin the color of old cavalry leather. He would never make a good poker player. Even in this deepening dusk, his eyes betrayed too much.

Hooker spoke in the easiest of tones. "Looking for me or Captain McCabe, were you?"

The man jerked his head. "Just lookin' around, sort of." There were tensions in his voice that made a farce of his forced grin. "Just out for some air," he said.

Continuing unhurriedly down the stairs, Travis Hooker nodded pleasantly. "It's a fine night, for a fact."

"That it is, sir," the trooper said, and bobbed his head emphatically. He shifted uncomfortably, then spoke in a blurting uneasiness. "Reckon I'd better get below, sir. If Captain Myles or Lieutenant Pryor caught me up here I'd be in for one hell of a chewing."

Hooker paused beside the man. He grinned knowingly. "I know just what you mean, friend, having been chewed out by some rebel officers in my time. Yankees or graybacks, they're all the same when they're wearing shoulder boards. No hard feelings, I hope, you and me having been on opposite sides of the fence?"

The trooper was beginning to feel more sure of himself; the strain was leaving his eyes. "Nope. Not any, sir. The war is over, I say."

"Over and done with, friend."

The trooper fidgeted, then drew a decisive breath of air. "Guess I'd better get back where I belong." But he kept standing there uneasily, as if waiting for permission to leave.

Travis Hooker's smile was slow and easy. "I suppose you're wondering what was going on between me and Captain McCabe."

"You and McCabe, sir?"

"He's over there by the pilot house."

The trooper's eyes were too roundly innocent, the tone of his voice too wholly guileless. "Why, I just now got here. I didn't see you and the captain over yonder. I just now got here, sir."

Hooker shrugged. "It doesn't matter, friend. Wasn't anything important. Come to think of it, I noticed you starting up the stairs about the same time I started down them."

"That's right, sir," the trooper said, and relief flooded into his eyes. "Same time, sir."

"Gambling man, are you, friend?" Hooker asked.

"Well, now..."

"I thought so," Hooker grinned. "I've never met a Yankee yet who wasn't handy with a deck of cards."

"I wouldn't go so far as to say..."

"And I've never met the trooper who didn't have an eye out for easy money," Hooker said, and nudged the trooper meaningly with his elbow. "Look, I know of a game you could clean up in, given you're interested. How about it, friend?"

"Now I don't know as I ought..."

"If you're short of cash, I'll stake you. We can split your winnings, if it'll make you feel better."

"Well, now..."

"Those roustabouts down below are loaded, amigo. They've got two months' pay in their pants, and no place to spend it. They're sheep just waiting to be sheared."

The trooper thought it over, tempted. Thirteen dollars a month didn't stretch very far, and he could use some extra cash. Maybe he could even hold out a little of the stake this Johnny Reb was offering to give him.

He was feeling surer of himself now. Keep on playing it as smart as he had so far, and he would end up with fresh money to spend and a corporal's stripes on his sleeve. He had overheard some damning evidence against this Travis Hooker, but he reckoned the telling could wait until after he had fleeced the rebel crew. It would make his story all the sweeter when he told how

Hooker had tried to cover up, tried to dull his suspicions or buy his silence with poker winnings. Touched up properly, it would furnish barracks gossip for months to come, Corporal Tim Hanrahan himself airing his exploit for the enlightenment of the rooks. "I could use some easy money, for a fact, sir."

"It'll be easier than you think," Travis Hooker told him.

They went down the stairs. On the main deck, they went past the long racks of stacked cordwood, past the engine house and boiler room. At the stern they halted. They were alone, and the light from the pine knots burning in the iron basket did not quite reach through the darkness to them. The trooper looked around.

"Where is that card game you were telling me about?" he asked.

The knife was sheathed under Travis Hooker's left arm, beneath his coat. He drew it with practiced swiftness. He drove the blade into the base of the trooper's throat, and there was no outcry.

The trooper arched to his toes, the thinnest of whispers escaping from his spasmed lips. An agonized whisper.

"God in heaven ... !"

Hooker put his hand against the man's chest, and shoved. The trooper went over the railing and into the water without a sound. For the briefest space of time his face was a contorted blur on the dark surface of the river. Then the currents caught him, turned him and carried him away.

When Hooker returned to the hurricane deck, Elise Casamore was still standing where he had left her. He looked around, toward the pilot house.

"Where is McCabe? He go below?"

Elise nodded mutely. Her lips moved, giving out no sound. They moved again, and her voice was a shallow whisper.

"Yes. To his cabin, I think. He was sick ... "

There was malice in Hooker's soft laughter. "He was easy. So big and powerful, and so damned easy to take apart!"

She did not ask him why he had done it, and he knew she would not ask. He stepped to her side, and glanced down toward the stern of the packet. He realized at once that she could not possibly have seen his execution of the Yankee trooper. Yet she knew. Two had walked along that narrow passageway below, and only one had returned. She knew what had happened as certainly as if she had witnessed it. Horror was in her eyes, the dredging sickness of shock.

He gazed steadily at her, smiling. "It's a beautiful night, isn't it?"

He heard the low, ragged intake of her breath, and it was not enough to satisfy him.

"I asked you a question, Miss Casamore," he said, his voice very pleasant and very insistent.

Her eyes were trapped on his; he would not let them escape. He waited patiently, magnifying the horror of his crime with his serene urbanity; he waited, amiably and inexorably, demanding an answer with the fear he was building up in her.

Her voice was the barest of whispers. "Yes."

He bowed slightly, mockingly. "So nice of you to agree," he murmured.

His tone of voice, pleasant as it was, held all the menace in the world. "You will never talk about anything but the weather from now on, Miss Casamore. Do you understand?"

"Yes ... yes."

The fear in her voice pleased him. It put a fine warm glow to the night and what it had brought him. He had made his move, and smashed aside all opposition. The way was open and clear for him now with the *Southern Belle* and what he intended to do, for fear, he had long ago learned, was the most potent of weapons.

He looked down at the girl, taking in the rounded symmetry of her breasts and the lines of her body with bold speculation.

"You're a very beautiful woman, you know," he told her with gentle malice. "I wouldn't want anything to ever happen to you, my dear."

He took a step closer to her. The railing behind her held her, trapped, unable to escape. He smiled down at her. He put his hand on the white column of her neck; he lowered his hand to the softness, the rounded woman's softness. Laughter rustled in his throat.

"One of these nights I'll send for you," he said.

He increased the pressure of his hand, fully aware that he was hurting her.

"When I do send for you," he told her, slowly and thinly, "be sure you come on the double. That is something else for you to remember from now on, Miss Casamore. When I'm in the notion for a woman, I never take it very kindly if she keeps me waiting."

CHAPTER EIGHT

Stripped to the waist in his quarters on the cabin deck, Branch McCabe stood gazing into the mirror at the image of a demolished man.

Except for a few small welts and faint discolorations, there were no marks on his face or body to tell of the misery that had been sledged into him. He had been worked over by an expert, and would carry hurts in him for days to come to remind him how unspeakably futile his own efforts had been.

There was a light rapping on his door, and Elise came into the room without waiting for his call. She closed the door behind her and stood watching him with sober concern.

"How do you feel?"

"There's only one way to describe it. Like pure hell."

She studied him somberly in the light of the cabin's bracket lamp, her gaze traveling over his bare chest and shoulders and arms. Her thoughts were easy enough to read, bringing a feeling of wry and weary amusement through McCabe's tattered pride.

"Sure, I know. Big as a mountain, and strong as an ox. But it wasn't enough this time, Elise. Not half enough. That fellow knows all the right moves. One wallop, and he had me wide open for the rest of it."

It was more than the girl could believe. "He must have taken you by surprise. He couldn't do it again."

McCabe shook his head moodily. "I've got a hunch he could do it just about any time he took the notion. Size isn't everything. Not when you meet up with the rare ones like Travis Hooker."

"What happened, Branch?"

McCabe's smile was thin and sour. "There appears to have been a difference of opinion on certain sundry matters pertaining to murder and sedition. Your Mister Hooker took it upon himself to convince me that I was wrong."

"And did he, Branch?"

"What he handed me I won't be likely to forget very soon."

There was nothing in Elise Casamore's nature that made impassiveness easy. She carried her emotions close to the surface of her eyes, and now a look of hurt and something that was close to bitter contempt came into them.

"No matter what you were during the war, the last thing I would have ever expected was to hear Branch McCabe admit that he was afraid."

He gazed at her soberly from across the small room, a girl who had invaded a man's harsh world and even now could not see what she was up against.

"The only people who aren't afraid of one thing or another are dead and in their graves, Elise," he told her quietly.

He picked up his shirt, and put it on. Small grimaces of pain ran through his face as he moved. He buttoned the shirt and stuffed the tails into his pants.

"Scared, Elise? I'm not ashamed to admit it. I've had beatings before, and can stand them again. But there are things happening on this boat that would scare any man."

She realized then how terribly unjust she had been. "I was wrong," she said simply. "I'm sorry, Branch."

His coat and cap were on the bed; turning, he went across the room to them. Elise's voice followed him.

"Everything you told me about my crew, I can believe now. What am I to do about them?"

"Not much you can do, Elise."

He heard the angry intake of her breath, as he wheeled around to face her. Protest was in her eyes, and in the cutting edge of her voice.

"Do you think I'm going to stand by and let them use my boat to get another war started?" she cried out at him. "I won't do it, Branch. Maybe you're afraid to fight them, but I'm not! I have no reason to love the North, but I will not allow my boat to be used to stir up another rebellion. I'll fire Travis Hooker. I'll fire every man in my crew."

"Try it," McCabe said meagerly. "They'd only laugh at you."

"I'll order the *Belle* back to St. Louis, then!"

McCabe smiled bleakly, wearily. "They'd kill me the instant I tried such a move," he said.

"You weren't afraid to turn against your own people when the war broke out," she snapped back angrily. "You weren't afraid of being called a turncoat, a traitor, when you felt that the Union was more important than slavery and a Southern Confederacy. Where are your fine, shining ideals now, Branch McCabe? Did you lose them in all the bottles you emptied? And your courage—did Travis Hooker's fists smash that out of you, too?"

"Take it easy, Elise."

"I see only what my eyes are showing me, Branch—a man who won't do what he can to prevent a new war simply because he's afraid of losing his own life."

McCabe murmured stonily, "You're right this much, Elise— I'm afraid of getting myself killed for no good at all."

"Then if you won't help me, I'll fight them alone," she said, flaring. "I'll go to Captain Myles. I'll tell him what Travis Hooker and my men are up to. I'll tell them everything. You were a turn-coat during the war. I'll become a turncoat to prevent a new war. I'm willing to become even more than that—an informer."

This, for Branch McCabe, was his greatest fear of all. "They'd kill you, Elise. Hooker warned me. He would kill you."

"My father and brother died fighting for what they felt was right. I'm a Casamore, too."

Temper flared up in McCabe, frustrated by this girl's blind and unyielding defiance. He walked across the room to where she stood, using his voice harshly on her.

"You won't do that, or any other damned thing. You listen to me, Elise. Travis Hooker is a killer. Rebellion is only an excuse. If it wasn't that, it would be something else. Men like him are born to be killers. You get in his way, he'll stomp you under with no more conscience than he felt when he shot down boys and old men during Quantrill's raids, and threw women and girls to the ground under him.

"I'll tell you what Hooker told me, Elise. He's got this boat fused for an explosion. You tip off his hand to the troopers, and he'll blow up this boat and everyone on it. Don't get the fool idea he was bluffing. Travis Hooker's kind don't bluff, ever. No matter where you or I go, he will have men nearby. You whisper, they'll hear you. You try to pass a written message, they'll see you. It's not only you and me who will die. It's the women and children you've got on board, and troopers who would be murdered without ever having any idea how or why. Do you want to carry a thing like that into eternity with you?"

"Dear Mother of God!" Elise whispered.

"So you are not going to say anything or do anything, understand?" McCabe told her bleakly. "This is a man's trouble, and you are going to stay out of it. No matter what I do, or what happens, you are going to stay out of it. You hear me, Elise?"

"Yes. Yes, Branch."

"Now get out of here, and never come back. Stay away from me. Whatever I do, I've got to do alone."

Elise was gone. McCabe put on his cap and coat, and went to the door. He paused there, his thoughts turning inward to grim issues. He was a man alone, and against Travis Hooker and the

Belle's hard-bitten crew he was like an ant struggling to move the boot that was poised to crush it. He was a man with a gun against his head, the hammer cocked and all the slack gone from the trigger.

I've got to find Hooker's powder cache. The harsh urgency of that thought sent him out of the cabin and along the promenade toward the stairs. He halted abruptly, suddenly realizing that this thing he had started out to do could be a fatal move.

Travis Hooker was no fool. Wherever McCabe went, eyes would follow him. It would be suicidal to start hunting for the hidden powder cache. Whatever he did in making his search of the packet, he would have to avoid the obvious. He would have to learn to think as Travis Hooker thought, slyly and craftily. He would have to do all his hunting with his eyes and his mind, while engaged in his routine chores and making his customary rounds as captain and pilot of the packet. Such methods would be appallingly slow, he realized bitterly, and his chances for success would be dismally meager. But there could be no hope at all, he knew, if he blundered rashly and got himself killed.

A voice spoke out of the darkness at one side. "Heading someplace, were you, Captain?"

McCabe turned. It was Lee Malvern moving toward him out of the night. Malvern's voice was dry and faintly mocking.

"Way you came out of your cabin and headed for the stairs, I'd say you had it in mind to go down to the main deck on some matter you considered mighty important. Change your mind of a sudden, did you?"

"I want a crew of wood cutters on the job first thing in the morning, Malvern."

The man's dry laughter rustled in the night. "Now was that all was crowding you so hard, Captain?"

"First thing in the morning. I want enough wood to carry us through a long run tomorrow."

McCabe turned on his heel and moved away from the grinning man. He drew a long slow breath, trying to ease off the cold tensions that had taken hold of him. That had been close, too close. In trouble like this, a man could make a single rash move and find himself suddenly dead.

Lee Malvern had not been standing there in the night for nothing. There would be others like him on the other decks, watching in the darkness. Travis Hooker had not been making an idle boast. His men were trained and organized, and they intended to allow nothing to come between them and the new and greater rebellion they meant to ignite in the South.

Moving across the deck, Branch McCabe's thoughts settled into somber channels. No matter how small, anything he did from now on that was out of the ordinary could bring swift disaster crashing down on him. His only hope was to never deviate from the normal routine that was expected of him. Eat, drink, sleep, work. He etched that pattern indelibly into his mind, shaping his future against Travis Hooker and the *Belle*'s die-hard rebels.

He had completed his day's work, and the time had not yet come for sleeping. The thing for him to do now was to have his supper.

The comforts of a river packet were few and crude, but in the combination saloon and dining room there was always a bright and shining magnificence, an elegance transported from more gracious places to a wild and dangerous corner of the frontier.

Here could be found warmth and the sparkle of gleaming lamps and glittering chandeliers. A bar ranged along the far wall, faced with ivory and rosewood inlays; above the bar, a great framed mirror added its own measure of dignity and grandness to the room. The bar was closed now, this being the hour for dining. All the tables were occupied.

Because he had been up the river many times before, Branch McCabe could look at each table and catalogue its occupants. It was always this way along the river. Cattlemen sought out the company of other cattlemen, and gamblers gravitated to their own kind when there was no game to occupy them; drummers inevitably drew together to exchange gossip of towns and commerce, and officers in army blue formed their own tight circle. No man sat alone.

In this room McCabe saw men who had abandoned good homes and fertile lands in order to join the unending rush toward Oregon and California, risking everything for the eternal dream of the restless. And in another year, he knew, most of those men would be traveling back to their former homes, beaten, disillusioned, bitter. It had been going on like this for twenty years now, and he wondered if it would ever end.

His gaze moved toward the corner table where sat drummers from Chicago and St. Louis, bound for the up-river settlements and mining camps to peddle their wares. Those booted, brown-faced ones over yonder were Texas men who could think only about vast herds of cattle flowing northward, and of free grass on a range where they would no longer be robbed and tormented by the carpetbaggers and Union Leaguers who were making life unbearable for the ex-rebels of the South.

The room held a hundred men who lived on as many different levels. Surveyors over there, and agents for the new railroad. Farmers, plainsmen and drifters. Men who hunted for sport, and those who hunted in order to live. Merchants and miners, traders, troopers, and card-sharps—the rich and the poor, the strong and the weak.

Sam Carthage, who was the packet's steward, crossed the room to where McCabe stood. Carthage had been one of Jo Shelby's specials during the war, McCabe remembered, and was never without the bulge of a hideout gun beneath his coat.

"Miss Casamore's compliments," Carthage said, and his eyes were bitter. "She asks would you care to join her at her table?"

McCabe looked across the crowded room, refusing to let Sam Carthage's obvious malice get into him. Elise, he saw, was seated at a table with Captain Myles and Lieutenant Pryor. Travis Hooker was there, too, a glint of derisive mockery playing in the cold depths of his tawny stare.

McCabe shook his head. "My gratitude and regrets to Miss Casamore," he said. "I want to pay a visit to the hospital room before I have my supper."

The gamble was too great, and he could not trust himself. Taking his food in the presence of Travis Hooker was an ordeal neither his pride nor his temper could stand up under.

CHAPTER NINE

TROOPER EMMETT REESE lay belly-down on the straw ticking, trying to take his mind from the pain of the bullet wound and mentally transposing the whorls in the planks of the wall into the lines of a girl's face.

Once he set his mind to it, it was possible to construct Lila's features in the swirled graining of the wood. The image that gradually took shape before his eyes lacked certain well-remembered details, but in his mind he filled in those missing contours and hues.

The red-brown sapwood was mighty close to the color of Lila's hair, he allowed. Given a slightly different turn in the pattern of the grain around that knot, and the shape of her chin and mouth would be next to perfect. The rest he filled in from memory: the tilt of her nose, the bantering vixen's eyes, the well-formed breasts.

For a moment, Trooper Emmett Reese almost forgot the blade that was probing into his flesh for the Sioux bullet, so lost was he in the image of Lila. An oval face she had, sweet as a lonely man's dream, with eyes laughing and teasing and tender, all at the same time. Lips as red as a Vermont apple picked on a frosty morning, only moist and warm and honey-sweet beneath his own when he kissed her, with her arms around him and her body close that last night they had been together. Such things a man could never forget, and would never want to forget.

The probe, digging into his rump for the bullet, struck a nerve, sweeping Lila's image away from him with a sudden spasm of pain.

"Double dee-damn, Doc!" the trooper blurted. "Leave a man something to sit on, can't you!"

"Hold still, boy."

"Ain't you got that slug out yet?"

"I think I'm down to it now."

"Like hell you are," Reese sighed. "That's my tailbone you're whittling on, sure as anything."

His eyes clamped shut, Trooper Reese summoned to mind every damnation he had ever heard, and aimed them one by one at the Sioux who had triggered this bullet into him.

Until now he had always felt a mite sorry for the Indians, losing their land and such, and being shoved from pillar to post by the whites. But not any more, by God! From this day on, he allowed he would be the hatingest man in Cady's Eleventh when it came to the Sioux.

It was a hell of a thing, and downright humiliating. All the fights he had been in, from Shiloh to these scratch-dirt Indian wars, he had never been hit before.

And when the bullet finally came with his name on it, it had to find its mark smack-dab in his butt!

Not that this was the worst. What graveled him even more was the fact that the slug, before finding his flesh, had torn thru his back pocket and demolished the one and only picture he had of Lila.

The door had opened; someone had come into the room. Trooper Reese twisted his head around, startled, thinking that all he needed right now to top off this whole goddam mess was for some clucking female to pop in and catch him belly-down like this, pants pulled down plumb to the knees, and not a stitch of underdrawers on.

But it was a man who had entered, the captain of the packet. Reese scowled.

"This is one hell of a thing, Cap."

"Tough," McCabe said.

The fellow sounded sincere enough, Emmett Reese decided, but that didn't help any. Even with the probe jabbing deeper and deeper into his buttock, pain and all, he could feel his face go red with outraged anger.

"Tough ain't the word for it," he snapped back savagely. "Hell a-mighty, Cap, you just don't know! I've got a girl waiting for me back in St. Louis, man. Promised her I'd come back a real for sure hero, I did. But what's she going to think when she finds out I caught a Sioux slug in my goddamn hiney?"

"Don't have to tell her, do you?"

"No?" Reese glowered. "Then how in blue blazes am I going to explain the bullet hole in her picture, I'd like to know?"

McCabe was trying not to grin.

Trooper Reese raged, and spent a fuming minute totally damning the Indian who had fired the shot.

"So now I've got to go out and get myself shot in the chest, that's what. Ain't nothing else I can do, b'God! Lila would chew me ragged if she ever found out I was carrying her picture in my hip pocket—instead of over my heart, like I promised."

The echoes of the trooper's wry humor followed Branch McCabe out of the hospital room and into the night. He wished that Clee Yandell and the others of the *Belle*'s rebel crew had been on hand to hear those lusty words. It might have opened their eyes and taught them a few things.

The spunky mettle and gritty humor of a fighting man! The graycoats of the South had not possessed it all.

He was moving along the promenade when several men came out of the darkness of the deck and halted him—Travis Hooker and Tully Kennerly, Creasey, Logart and Lou Savaine. It was this man Savaine, McCabe thought dismally, whose skill with a knife had earned him his murderous reputation while riding with Quantrill's guerrillas on Missouri's dark and bloody frontier.

They blocked him off and crowded him aside, pinning him against the deck railing. No talk or wasted effort. Their maneuver was quick and smoothly efficient, carried out in the stark malevolence of complete silence. They knew all the trickery, these rebel die-hards, all the sharp and deadly ways. Men had been stationed at both ends of the promenade to prevent escape or interference.

This, Branch McCabe knew, was how death could come to him from the packet's renegade crew, and he watched them closely, wondering drearily if they had marked him for execution tonight.

"Been waiting for you," Travis Hooker said.

"Obvious enough," McCabe answered. He had known fear before, and the roughshod rashness of defiant temper. He held both under stern control now, measuring this gaunt minute and what it might hold for him. A single prayer stood hard and brittle in his mind, that he could take at least one of them with him before he went under. Just one of them—Travis Hooker. But he would have only his hands to do that for him, and his hands, he knew, would not be enough.

Hooker's smile was thin as a knife blade. "Your concern for the welfare of bluecoat troopers strikes us as being a shade out of line, McCabe."

"So?"

"You have a short memory, it seems," Hooker told him. "A very short memory, McCabe."

Lou Savaine's right hand was restlessly rubbing the wrist of his left. There was a stiletto sheathed just inside the cuff of that sleeve, a slim and vicious weapon. The man's gaze was one of impassionate speculation, cold and unblinking in the dim starshine of the night.

"A fatally short memory, I might say," Travis Hooker breathed.

The threat was there, the dire and deadly promise. McCabe shook his head slowly. "Not as short as you seem to think," he said, and wondered if his voice sounded as thin and tight to these hard-eyed men as it did to him. "I haven't forgotten a thing."

"Strange way you've got of showing it, fretting about the health of a few gunshot Yankees."

"Now hold on a minute…"

"Show him, Savaine."

The knife was suddenly in Lou Savaine's hand, the tip of it biting into the base of McCabe's throat. He stood very still, scarcely breathing, for Savaine was a man who relished such things as this.

Travis Hooker's voice was a shallow whisper through the darkness. "One quick jab would do it. Less than an inch more, and not a sound to tell of your dying. I warned you, McCabe."

"So I remember."

"You don't think we'd do it?"

"I have no doubt that you'd do it."

"Just asking for it, then?" Hooker breathed, softly and savagely. "Is that why you went to see about those wounded Yankees? Just to show me that you're big and brave, and don't give a damn about what I told you up on the hurricane earlier tonight?"

"I'm not that brave," McCabe said. He breathed slowly. "Neither am I entirely a fool."

"Now what is that supposed to mean?"

"Open your eyes, man, and have a look at what you've been showing to the Yankees on this boat. Your men ganging up on those two troopers the other day. Yandell, Malvern, and the others with a chip on their shoulders all the time. And you've been almost as transparent most of the time."

Temper came spilling into Hooker's eyes, hot and wicked, and against it Branch McCabe spoke with far more brashness than he felt.

"You're smart, Hooker, but this is one time you're not thinking straight. If you were, you'd be in that sickroom right now trying to make Myles and Pryor think you want nothing more than to see those wounded troopers pull through. You've been acting like a kid with his hand stuck in a candy jar, trying to steal a few small pieces when he could get away with the whole works."

Lou Savaine increased the pressure of the stiletto against McCabe's throat.

"It would go in quick and easy," the man said, his voice soft as a woman's. "Less than an inch to go, and you don't talk big any more."

Travis Hooker's stare was flat, demanding. "What are you driving at, McCabe?"

"Not until you've told this butcher to put his knife away."

Savaine's eyes went small and mean.

"Put it away," Hooker told the man.

"So now he's giving the orders!"

Hooker spoke without moving his lips. "God damn you, Lou, do as I told you."

He lowered the knife. With his back against the railing of the deck, McCabe fixed his eyes on Travis Hooker.

"Ever since we left St. Joe, you and your men have been acting exactly like what you are—rebel hotheads itching to make trouble. A certain amount of that the Yankees expect and will put up with. Give them too much, though, and you'll bring them down on you like a runaway wagon. You'll be finished on this river before you ever get started."

There was a movement in the darkness beyond Hooker and his men. It was Elise, standing in the doorway of her cabin. McCabe thrust her out of his mind. She no longer mattered. Nor did he himself matter, for even if he won this grim and deadly gamble there could be no complete victory. Not for him. He was a man wagering all that he was and ever hoped to be on winds that were hot and wild and merciless, and even if victory came to him he would find nothing for himself but the bitterness of futility and loss.

Travis Hooker was smiling sardonically. "Guess it doesn't take as much as I figured to give you the cure."

He gave those words plenty of time to sink their sting into McCabe, then said, "You're beginning to act like a man changing his coat for the second time. Southerner to Yankee, and now Southerner again. A regular human chameleon, you are. I'm a little disappointed in you, McCabe."

"Don't make any wrong guesses about me, Hooker."

"Well, now!"

"I'm fed up with politics and crusades," McCabe told the man savagely. "Ideals I can do without. All I ever got for mine was thirteen dollars a month, and every dirty name a man can be called. From now on, I'm thinking about no one but Branch McCabe."

"Another brother of Judas," Hooker murmured dryly. "Another man with his price."

"Ten thousand dollars is mine," McCabe answered coldly. "And every time you try to rawhide me, the price gets jacked up another notch."

Hooker snorted. "You overrate yourself, mister. I warned you about getting bucky with me. Maybe I'll let Savaine have you after all."

"Maybe. But I don't think you will."

Hooker let a derisive half smile build up through the temper that was in his eyes. "You seem mighty damned sure of yourself. I'm curious just what gives you this sudden notion that you're so indispensable."

"I'll give it to you with the hair on, Hooker. We're in Sioux country, two hundred miles in the middle of nowhere. The channels that were open today will be changed by tomorrow. Sandbars move around, and there will be snags and sawyers tomorrow where there weren't any today. Eliminate me, and where will you find another pilot who knows this river?"

Travis Hooker answered with more bluff than conviction. "Malvern has been up here before. He could do it."

McCabe looked at the man. "Well?"

Lee Malvern feared neither God nor man, but he knew his limitations. He shook his head slowly. "I guess not."

Hooker thought about it for another moment, then spoke shortly. "McCabe, you're out of your head if you think I've got that kind of money."

"You'll have it when the time comes. Yankee dollars."

The eyes narrowed, cold and unreadable as they studied Branch McCabe closely. "And when will that be?"

He was beyond turning back now, beyond retreat. "When I give you a regiment of Yankee dead," McCabe answered steadily. "When I give you what you'll need to start off your new rebellion."

Travis Hooker and his men were gone, and McCabe stood at the door of Elise's cabin. He didn't knock. When she opened the door again, as he knew she would, her face was pale in the night, and around her eyes and mouth was a look of utter loathing.

"Thirty pieces of silver, and the man who sold his soul for them," she said scornfully.

"More than that," McCabe corrected, and smiled stonily. "Ten thousand of them, Elise."

"Exactly ten thousand more than you are worth," she told him, her voice thin and cutting. She gazed at him as though seeing him for the very first time. "How tall are you, Branch? Six-feet-two? Six-four? It means nothing. No... you are really a very small man, Branch McCabe. Quite contemptibly small and disgustingly shallow."

"A man does what he has to do, Elise."

"The apology of the corrupt and cowardly!"

McCabe shrugged.

"Twice a traitor," she murmured stingingly. "Twice a Judas!"

Just looking at him seemed to sicken her; she stepped back and started to shut the door on him, but he blocked it with his foot.

He let his anger show. "This is a man's trouble you bought into, Elise, and what you saw and heard here tonight is no affair of yours. You hear me? And don't bother yourself with any woman's notions about trying to change things and make a better man of me. I know what I want, and how to go about getting it."

"Yes. It is quite obvious that you do."

"What you think about me doesn't matter, not at all. Only don't ever show it, you hear? Treating me like dirt could make the Yankees suspicious, and that is one thing I won't put up with from you. Nor would Travis Hooker, either. You remember that, Elise. Don't you ever forget it."

"I'm not afraid of you, Branch McCabe."

"Then you'd better be doubly afraid of one Travis Hooker. You get in the way, and he'll make you regret the day you were born."

He turned abruptly away from her, walking heavily. He was a big man, a towering man. But what he had taken upon himself this night was a burden that could crush and destroy even the strongest of men.

Inside her cabin, Elise Casamore sat on the edge of her bed, staring numbly at the paneled wall. The echoes of Branch's bleak promise to Travis Hooker still rolled starkly and terribly through the corridors of her mind.

A regiment of Yankees dead! It was as though she could look into each grave, and see Branch McCabe standing above them all in the guilt of his crime.

She tried to tell herself that he had not really meant what he had said, that he could not possibly mean it.

But what else was there for her to believe, she asked herself bitterly, except what she had heard and what he had told her?

CHAPTER TEN

Fort Abraham Lincoln lay loose and sprawling on the bend of the river not far below the town of Bismarck, its bleached walls and battlements showing the scars of many attacks by Indian hostiles.

During the four days since the *Southern Belle* had nosed in at the landing and secured its shore lines, Branch McCabe had come to realize for the first time the full magnitude of the campaign that was to be made this year against the Sioux.

The wide raw streets of Bismarck were crowded with wagon trains being packed and outfitted for the long and dangerous haul overland to Forts Ellis and Fetterman. A constant confusion of traffic cluttered the streets and flowed in and out of the town—troopers, plainsmen, traders and settlers caught in the vortex of an action that fused all lives into its own grim mold.

At night the saloons howled and the gambling dens thrived, and lamps blazed bright and bold in the parlors of brothels. Men labored in sweat and gambled with their blood, for there was no knowing what tomorrow would bring. McCabe would not permit Elise to remain in town unescorted after dark, for on those wild streets were dangers no prudent man would dare risk.

This campaign was to be no mere punitive action against the Sioux, as in years past. Of this Branch McCabe became increasingly more certain during the days the *Belle* lay tied in at the landing. General Sevier's plans were being made with inexorable care, and smacked of a war of major proportions.

In McCabe were memories of many battles not long past, the swift probing skirmishes and the massive actions that called for shrewd scheming and a careful build-up of supplies. The pattern in what he was witnessing now was old and familiar. This campaign was intended to destroy the power of the Sioux once and for all time.

There was gossip making the rounds in Bismarck and Fort Lincoln that General Canaday had moved out with his column almost two months ago, had surprised and destroyed a village of the Ogalalla Sioux. Then word came that Bear-Stands-Up had rallied his warriors with unexpected savagery, and forced Canaday to retreat. The destruction of the Ogalalla village turned out to be a costly victory, for now it was known that Red Moon, Crazy Wolf and Bloody Hand, infuriated by the attack, had painted for war.

A host of rumors ran through the hills and along the river. McCabe gave thought to them all, rejecting the obvious fabrications of barracks gossip, and accepting only the information which seemed logical and sound. On these probabilities, he began drawing together his own plans.

According to the talk, General McKinn was moving his force down the Yellowstone, and was to join General Turley near the mouth of Glendive Creek, at Stanley's Stockade. Then a courier reached Fort Lincoln soon after with information that Canaday's column had once again moved northward out of Fort Fetterman, and had been struck on the Tongue River by the Ogalalla warriors under Bear-Stands-Up. Another battle had raged over the hills and ravines, and once again Canaday had been forced to retire from the field to escape annihilation.

Never before had the Sioux been known to fight with such stubborn ferocity. In Bismarck's saloons and gambling dens grizzled freighters indicated a moody foreboding as they told about smoke signals rising from the hills around the Powder and Big Horn Rivers, and of Arickaree scouts reporting that the Cheyennes were now adding their might to the powerful Sioux. The massacre at Sand Creek was being remembered this year as never before by the hostiles. And hard-bitten veterans squatting on their heels in the barracks or behind the rifle butts at Fort Lincoln, allowed that the wanton destruction of Kettle's village on the Washita by Cady's Eleventh would be paid for in full by bluecoat troopers before this year's campaign was over and done.

Branch McCabe spent long hours studying the map tacked to the wall of his cabin.

Two hundred or more miles to the southwest was Fort Fetterman, from which Canaday's troops were making their probing actions to the north. Out yonder, farther to the west, was the place they had once called Coulter's Hell, the headwaters of the Yellowstone. He traced the line of the river until he located Fort Ellis, and now the full picture of the campaign began taking shape in his mind.

With McKinn's column marching east along the Yellowstone, and General Turley's force moving west out of Lincoln to intersect Canaday's command, the jaws of a giant three-pronged trap would close on the Sioux somewhere between the Big Horn and Powder Rivers.

This fact became increasingly clear to Branch McCabe during the days the *Belle* lay tied in at the landing. And there was more. A campaign of this magnitude required great stores of provisions. Wagon trains would of course be used, but they were tediously slow and vulnerable to attack by the hostiles.

The Yellowstone River and Elise Casamore's packet, therefore, offered the only practical solution to General Sevier's problem of supply, McCabe reasoned grimly, and that night he was given to understand that Travis Hooker also shared this conviction.

Hooker's orders to McCabe and Elise were blunt. "When Sevier asks to contract for this boat, you let him have it. Don't argue price. No matter what he offers, you let him have it. I've got a few things in mind for his bluecoats that he won't be bargaining for."

Later that night, alone in his cabin, McCabe stood in brooding silence. He felt like a man lashed to a powder keg. The fuse was burning, and there was nothing at all he could do to put it out.

CHAPTER ELEVEN

HIS NAME WAS Jubal, a huge man with smooth mahogany skin and no idea at all how old he was. It had always troubled him that he could not count the number of his years. In a dim way he could recollect a home in another land, somewhere across an endless world of water and empty sky. The picture was like a shadow lying far back in Jubal's mind, of the face of the woman who had been his mammy, and then of white men coming with guns and whips and of unending days on a boat that smelled of grime and the rankness of sweat. His mammy had died on that boat, he remembered.

He didn't know how long ago that had happened, but he allowed it must be nigh onto thirty years, maybe more. He had worked for Marse Heddings for almost twenty years, after being sold by Marse Beauregard when he was about as tall as middling high sugar cane at cutting time.

Anybody asked Jubal, he always said he was thirty years old. But in his own mind he was never sure. All he knew for a fact was that there was gray showing up at his temples nowadays, and maybe that was a sign he had more years than only thirty. He wished he knew for certain. He didn't know why it seemed so important, except that when a man got old and died it didn't seem proper somehow if he couldn't leave folks the right number of years to put on his marker.

During the long hours of day, Jubal worked alongside the common roustabouts of the *Southern Belle,* even though as boss stoker he might have been able to avoid much of the drudgery of loading firewood onto the packet.

But in his mind it was less bother to do the work than try to get out of it, and it always prided him to single out the strongest of the roustabouts and then humble the man with the huge weights of wood he could tote. Today, Jubal allowed he had given Big Tom a few things to think about, and maybe from now on the fellow would stop being so braggish about being the most man of them all on the *Belle*.

The work of the day now done, Jubal got his tin plate and cup and took his place at the head of the line, feeling pleasure at the dignity of this distinction he had earned for himself.

Not many darkies ever won the job of being boss stoker on a boat, for mostly it was white folks who were given that important chore. When he got home again, one of the first things his woman would ask him to tell her about was how he had to give orders for wood to be lugged up when it was time for stoking the fire-boxes, and how he had to help Clee Yandell keep a close eye on the steam gauge to be sure the pressure in the boilers never built up to the danger point.

His cup filled and tin plate heaped, Jubal squatted on his heels and took his food. Yes, Melinda would sure enough start asking questions first thing he got home again and settled down. The thought was a warm one in Jubal's mind—almost like she was right there on the *Belle* with him. He could picture her sitting in her favorite chair with young Sam and Jed and Sari Lou on the floor close beside her, their eyes big as Yankee dollars as they listened to the stories he would yarn.

Jubal smiled as he ate. Closing his eyes, he could call to mind so real-like it was almost scarey when he thought about it—the clicking of Melinda's knitting needles, slow and easy when he was just starting to talk, then clickety-clacking like hens on a tin roof when he got to the exciting places, her eyes watching his face all the while and maybe smiling a little now and then as though she was secretly knowing all the things he was telling her weren't the honest-to-God whole truth.

And Jubal knew that like as not he'd make up some of the things he'd tell his woman. It would give Melinda a mite of extra pleasure to recollect them over and over in her mind when he was gone again. A woman expected her man to get braggity a little. Not sinful-like, but at least enough to come up to the way she thought of him. A woman always thought of her man as bigger, stronger and braver than he actually was, and it was only right and proper, Jubal allowed, for him to try to fit the image she held of him in her mind.

Only he was doubtful how wise it was for his children to hear too much yarning about how important their pappy was. Might give them biggety notions when they grew up. In Jubal's mind, it wasn't fitting for darkies to act uppish around white folks, even if Old Abe and his Yankee army had set them free.

His meal finished, Jubal dropped his plate and cup into the wreck pan, and made his way along the deck to the packet's rounded prow. Behind him several of the roustabouts were settling down to another game of *vingt-et-un* under the guttering light of pine knots burning in one of the iron baskets near the engine room. Jubal allowed he didn't feel much like gambling tonight, and when he considered setting out a trot line to catch a mess of fish, that idea didn't take hold in him either.

A nagging restlessness had been building up in him ever since the *Belle* had tied in here at the Fort Lincoln landing, and at the core of it was always Melinda. He couldn't get her out of his thoughts.

It wasn't right, he told himself moodily, for a man to have to be away from his woman such a long spell when there were hankerings in him that only she could relieve. It was times like this when Jubal found himself close to hating Old Abe for making him a free man. His life had never been so pestered and miserable before the war, when he had been owned.

As he looked out into the darkness of the night he could see Melinda so plain and clear that it brought a torment of aching hunger into him—the dusty prettiness of her face, the sound of her voice, the rounded warmth of her that he knew so well.

He turned away abruptly, the restlessness fretting his nerves until he could no longer stand it. One of the men looked up from the game, waving a deck of dogeared cards at him.

"How's about settin' in, Jubal? We could use some new money in this yere game."

Jubal shook his head. "Don't feel of a mind for it, Lafe."

Big Tom was eyeing him speculatively, the muscles of his huge shoulders bunching and loosening beneath his sweat-stained shirt.

"Jubal, let's you and me fight."

Jubal gazed moodily at the man.

Big Tom grinned widely. "You proved today you're the most man when it comes to totin' firewood," he said, "and now I'm wonderin' if you're the most man in a fight. One ain't always same as the other, way I see it. How's about fightin' me, boy?"

Jubal studied the man soberly. "For fun, or for real?"

There was no malice in Big Tom's dark face as he chuckled. "For fun, boy—only for fun. Just 'cause you're a stud horse for work ain't no call for me to feel mean at you. It'll be just a nice, friendly fight, Jubal."

He stood up slowly, a squat, powerful man with the shoulders of a bayou bull, grinning amiably at Jubal and flexing his long arms as he waited. Jubal studied the man speculatively, trying to call up that hot, surging excitement that had always before swept through him at times of challenge. But it wouldn't come. He shook his head with moody regret.

"Guess I ain't of a mind for fightin' tonight, Big Tom."

"Tomorrow night, boy?"

Jubal nodded. "Feel more like it tomorrow night, maybe," he said, and walked on.

He halted again, staring down at the Missouri's dark currents, all of a sudden fed up with the river and the packet and everyone on it, most of all himself.

He knew what was wrong with him. He needed a woman. Not just any woman, but Melinda. As he thought of her the distance between them suddenly became a crushing, overpowering thing that threatened to tear him apart, and he heeled sharply around and went tramping along the deck to the engine room.

He shoved aside the rolled-up straw ticking, knowing there was no use trying to sleep. He dug a clean shirt and fresh pair of pants out of the canvas bag and changed into them. He reached behind the chest of tools to the hiding place where he kept his money and took out four silver dollars. Straightening, he stepped outside again, and at once found himself the target for the ribald joshing of the roustabouts loafing nearby.

"How's come you're all fixed up, Jubal? Where you goin', man?"

"Ain't no one gets himself all fancied up middle of the week without he's aimin' on some tomcatting. Want me to tell you a mighty good place to go to, Jubal?"

He swung angrily away, pestered by the rowdy laughter of the men. Their jibes followed him as he went lunging across the lowered staging and up the river bank.

"... two-bit house right behind the livery yards, Jubal. I hear tell there's a black gal in there ... "

Jubal strode on, almost running.

He came to Bismarck, and made his way uncertainly along the wide, wheel-rutted street, feeling alone and lonely. He wished now that he hadn't come, but he knew he couldn't go back to the packet this early in the night and face the roughneck humor of the roustabouts.

The Almighty Lord had never created a bigger fool, he told himself moodily, than a man homesick for his woman.

He went slowly along the plank walk, hesitating at each saloon and gambling den, then moving restlessly on. He came to the livery yard and there he halted, staring through the night toward the dimly-lighted windows of the house that sat far back on a weedy lot, thinking about the girl whose skin was the same color of his own, who worked in that place.

Lu-Ann, someone had said her name was. And Jubal found himself remembering all the jokes he had heard about whites going to her, for a change of luck. He reckoned sourly that she'd find his money just as good as any other man's, and he took a determined stride toward the house.

But he halted, realizing all at once that he couldn't go through with it. There was a difference, and he didn't know what it was. All he knew for sure was that the image of Melinda kept rising like magic between him and the house, and that no other woman could ever take her place, not even for a short time. *I'm gonna get myself good and drunk,* he told himself savagely, and turned back down the street.

He came to the general store and saw Miss Elise inside, several small packages under her arm, with Travis Hooker standing close by. Jubal walked on. He went past the hotel, and stopped at the first saloon he came to.

He stepped close to the window and peered through, a little awed by the glittering lamps and the great back-bar mirror, the frame of which gleamed like real gold.

He recognized Lieutenant Stacey, who had traveled up the river from St. Joe on the *Belle.* Beyond him along the ornate bar stood Colonel Maxwell Cady with several other bluecoat officers. Cady cut a dashing figure in his long flowing mustache and striking uniform, swirling gold braid and buttons polished to a fare-thee-well, and a bright red neckerchief knotted under his collar. A fine-looking gentleman, Jubal thought, and remembered how this Yankee officer had torn rebel lines apart at Yellow Tavern, Five Forks, and a score of other bitter engagements during the war.

Jubal stepped back from the window. A place as grand as this was not for the likes of him, even if he was boss stoker on the *Belle,* no matter what fine words Old Abe had orated about all men being the same, black or white.

He walked on. Near the edge of town he came to a saloon that offered no ornate pretenses. Through this window he could see teamsters and Yankee troopers crowding a small smoky room, drinking at the bar or gambling at the tables. The confusion of loud voices and heavy laughter made a tumultuous sound against the night.

Jubal stuck a hand into his pocket and palmed the four silver dollars. He was nagged by a growing indecision, not rightly knowing if he ought to go into the place. He had never dared do such a thing back home. But maybe it was different up here. He wasn't an owned man any more, he reminded himself. Maybe what Old Abe had said, and all the fighting the Yankees had done had changed things. Maybe it was fitting now for him to go into a saloon and buy whisky just like anyone else with a thirst on.

He turned away from the window, and went to the cut-away doors. He hesitated a moment, once again mulling the matter over uneasily. Then, a little amazed at himself, he found himself pushing the doors open and stepping inside. He was conscious of faces turning toward him, of eyes staring at him. But no one shouted for him to get out.

The room had been an uproar of voices and heavy laughter, but now Jubal became aware of a silence taking over the place, spreading along the bar and from table to table until all at once the hush was complete.

And he was conscious of hard faces staring at him, and of the man behind the bar swinging around to find the reason for the silence. The man was medium-tall and thick-necked, with shoulders so powerfully rounded beneath his shirt that he looked humped. Jubal thought he saw temper flare up in the man's eyes, and all of a sudden he wanted to pivot and get out of the place.

Then one of the troopers at the bar spoke up mildly. "Come alive, Mike. You've got a customer here."

Jubal hesitated. He allowed that he'd been wrong about the bartender being riled at the sight of him because the man's eyes seemed placid enough now. And the voice sounded friendly enough.

"I'm Mike O'Hara, boy. Come in, come in! What can I do for you, now?"

Jubal shifted uneasily. "I just thought maybe y'all would be kind enough to sell me some whisky, please, suh," he said.

One of the troopers at the bar grinned slowly, saying, "You'll have to speak louder if you want Mike to hear you. He's kind of deaf."

And O'Hara boomed at him from behind the bar. "Talk louder, boy. I'm stone deaf."

Jubal raised his voice a notch through the silence of the room. "I'd like to buy some whisky, if you please, suh. I've got cash money in my pocket."

"Can't hear a word you say!" O'Hara bellowed back at him. "I'm deaf, I tell you. You want something here, boy, don't whisper about it."

Jubal raised his voice another notch through the room's staring hush. He was shocked at the loudness of his own words. It wasn't seemly, he thought, for him to be hollering like this among white folks.

"Please, suh, will you kindly sell me a bottle of whisky? I've got cash money to pay for it."

O'Hara raised his big hands, waggling his fingers for Jubal to come closer. "Nearer, boy. I couldn't hear thunder from where you are."

Jubal hesitated, then moved deeper into the room, toward the bar. Uncertainty halted him again, but O'Hara's hands urged him closer. When he was at the bar he started to speak again, but the man shook his head.

"Night like this, I couldn't hear a cannon go off. I'll come around there, boy."

He came lumbering around the end of the bar, and all of a sudden the silence of the room was a thing of fearsome torment for Jubal. He wished bitterly he hadn't come here, and it was in his mind that maybe all these eyes staring at him was the punishment the good Lord handed out to men like himself who were foolish enough to forget their rightful place. Like the Lord bringing down His wrath on Adam. A man hankering to get drunk just because he was homesick for his woman was wrong and sinful, he thought dismally. He started to turn away toward the door.

But O'Hara was close in front of him now, between him and the door, a blocky bear of a man with short thick arms and deep, powerful shoulders.

"Now, what was that you were saying?" The man's voice boomed at him. "Speak up, boy, if you want me to hear you."

Jubal's voice was a loudness that shocked his own ears. "A bottle of whisky, please, suh. I got cash money to pay for it."

Through that silence, his words seemed to fill the entire room and come crashing back at him. He heard a ripple of laughter run through the place; he saw O'Hara's face go ruddy with released temper, and he heard the man's voice crack out at him, low and harsh with wrath.

"Who the hell you think you're yelling at, fellow?"

Jubal realized then that all this had been one vicious jest, and a feeling of sudden panic swept through him. He tried to grin, making an empty gesture with his hands, a groping apology.

"Why, suh, I thought you said ... " It occurred to him that his voice was still overly loud. He tried to lower it to a proper level. "For a fact, suh, I thought ... "

O'Hara's shoulder heaved forward, driving his fist into Jubal's belly.

The man's voice was thick with fury and contempt. "I'll teach the likes of you never to raise your voice to me," he said, and slammed his second blow home. It hurt. The impact of those two blows spilled pure agony through Jubal, and he turned and fell against the bar. O'Hara hit him again. Jubal stood there, head down and gagging for breath. His hands were flat on the bar below his face. He stared numbly at them. The palms were paler than the rest of his skin, almost like those of a white man's. In a dull, slack way he found himself remembering the time when he was a boy when he had tried to scrub all the darkness out of his skin, using sand and lye soap and scrubbing and scrubbing…

O'Hara's fist sledged the small of his back, the impact of it spinning him around in a spasm of agony. He heard the laughter of troopers fill up the room until it was like a thundering uproar crashing around him.

"Maybe that'll teach you and your kind never to come into my place again," O'Hara said harshly, and drove his fist to Jubal's face.

In an unthinking numbness, Jubal drew his head back, missing the blow. The momentum of Mike O'Hara's swing threw him off balance, and he fell. He swore thickly, shoving himself up from the floor in an explosive flare of rage. Panic swept through him then, and he heard O'Hara roar out his fury as he went lunging past him toward the door, thinking only of escape.

It was the outthrust boot of one of the troopers that tripped him. He pitched headlong through the cutaway doors, sprawling on the plank walk outside. He was conscious of men rushing out of the saloon behind him. He was on his feet and trying to get away when O'Hara came at him again, driving hard, sledging blows to his face and body. He backed away from the man, trying futilely to shield himself from those heavy blows smashing at him. But O'Hara had pinned him against the wall of the saloon; he couldn't escape.

He heard a girl's angry cry. "Stop hitting that man!" It was, he somehow knew, Miss Elise's voice. "Stop it, I said!"

Mike O'Hara stopped. Jubal took his arms away from his face. He could taste blood in his mouth. Pain throbbed behind his eyes in rhythmic thumping explosions that unsteadied his sense of balance and blurred his vision. He could make out Elise

Casamore standing in the light of the window, staring at the saloonman with furious contempt. The scope of Jubal's vision was widening...now he could make out Travis Hooker a short distance away, his gaze alert.

Jubal rocked his head around until he was looking at the saloonman. Mike O'Hara was eyeing the girl with grinning boldness, and now there was a rustle of dry laughter rising from the Yankee troopers behind the saloon owner.

Jubal felt his first heat of resenting wrath as he looked at those men. Wasn't right, what they were showing in their eyes as they watched the girl. Miss Elise wasn't trash. She was real quality.

He heard her lash out at O'Hara with angry scorn. "It must take a world of courage to beat up a man who is making no attempt at all to defend himself."

Mike O'Hara's grin spread wider and wider. "Now, lady, I'm real sorry if I happened to do some damage to your personal property. This here fellow does belong to you, doesn't he?"

Against the night, the girl was like a pale flame standing in anger and defiance. It made Jubal prideful, just seeing her as she was, and it also made him afraid.

"Jubal is his own man," he heard her say, and her voice was like the cutting edge of a blade. "Is this the kind of treatment you Yankees give a man after fighting a war to set him free?"

O'Hara's gaze was warm and humid. It traveled the lines of the girl's body with mocking boldness, and now he mused insolently, "You're a feisty little rebel, ain't you? Now if it's another slave you want, sweetie, how's about giving me a chance?"

Swift fury swept through her face, and she struck him a stinging blow with the flat of her hand. O'Hara caught her wrist in his big hand, laughing roughly as he yanked her against him, then spun her and thrust her away with a snort of derision.

Jubal heard her small cry of pain as she stumbled and fell. A sudden overpowering wrath broke loose through him that moment, and for the first time in his life he made no effort to check it.

He lunged forward, grunting softly as he drove his fist to the shelf of O'Hara's jaw. He followed it instantly with a second blow that carried all the weight of his huge shoulders. He knew as Mike O'Hara went down that the man would not get up again, for he had heard the sound of bones letting go under that chopping smash to O'Hara's jaw.

Then he saw the troopers coming at him in a solid rush. He leaped back, planting his shoulders against the wall of the saloon. In him that moment was a hot and storming hatred for all Yankees who would torment a blameless man and make bold with the girl who had defended him.

Jubal waited. He let the troopers come to him, making no effort at all to escape. Never before had he felt so big and strong and unbridled. He sledged down the nearest man with one massive fist, and smashed the next one aside with a single mighty blow. He realized he could not hope to beat off such overwhelming odds, but in him was a great soaring joy that was like the singing of angels as he drove his blows home.

The sheer weight of their numbers held him pinned against the wall. He was conscious of hands beating and tearing at him, of boots kicking and bent knees ramming viciously at his vital area. He caught two men with his great hands, and cracked their heads together. He hurled them away from him and stood there with his back to the wall, bucking, beating, slugging. There were men smashed down by him who were showing no ready inclination to rejoin the battle. And that was the glory in Jubal's mind even as the certainty deepened in him that he was taking a brutal beating that could cripple or kill him.

A man leaped at him, trying to ride him to the ground. He shook the fellow off with a heave of his shoulders, and pitched him away with a slashing backhand blow. There was a great consuming weakness spreading through him now, eroding the impact of his fists. He thought it a bit odd that he could no longer feel much pain in the jolting blows of the troopers.

He was dimly aware of other men rushing along the street toward him, and he heard a lawman's whistle cut through the uproar of voices with its shrill, stabbing cry.

Someone hit him on the head with a gun barrel, then clubbed him a second time. He was down without knowing when he had fallen. He was aware of the rough planks of the board walk beneath his cheek. He saw the boots of a trooper close by; he watched one of them lift and then slam violently against his ribs.

He heard himself groan a soft protest. Then the night and all the world came crashing down on him, and he knew no more.

It was early morning when Branch McCabe came to the jail, paid Jubal's fine and led him outside. His body was one great throbbing ache, and it was in his mind that nothing pleased a man quite so much after the punishment of a brawl as the warmth of the good Lord's sun.

Outside, McCabe turned and regarded him with sober interest, speaking slowly. "Jubal, you look like the wrath of God."

"It's how I feel, Cap'n. It purely is."

McCabe's mouth bent in the faintest of smiles. "Man, that must have been a fight to behold! You gave this town something to remember, last night."

Jubal shook his head regretfully. "I cost you money to get me out, did I?"

"Worth every cent of it, Jubal, what you did."

"I didn't go to discommode you, Cap'n. But when that O'Hara man laid his hands on Miss Elise … "

"He'll be a long time doing a thing like that again."

They turned down the street, making for the river landing. A trio of troopers was loafing on the liar's bench in front of the Plainsmen's saloon, and one of them grunted derisively as they approached.

McCabe paused. The three men were husky enough to make serious trouble. He looked at them in serious challenge. He waited until the derision in their eyes was replaced by a look of uneasy reconsideration, then he touched Jubal's arm and they moved on.

At the edge of town Jubal halted, rummaging back through his hazy memory of the brawl. "I seem to recollect someone sidin' me just afore I went down, Cap'n. That was Mistah Hooker, was it?"

McCabe shook his head. "He never raised his hand. It was a Yankee officer who pulled that mob off you, and it cost him some lumps to do it. Lieutenant Pryor."

Jubal shook his head, puzzled. It had been bluecoat troopers who had ganged up on him, but he allowed it wasn't fair for him to tar them all with the same brush. Yankees like Lieutenant Stacey Pryor were real quality.

Which was a sight more than he could say for Travis Hooker.

CHAPTER TWELVE

Well, the step has been taken, McCabe told himself grimly, *and there's no turning back now.*

The agreement had been reached, the papers signed. For the sum of three hundred and fifty dollars per day, General Turley was to have the services of the *Southern Belle* during this campaign against the Sioux hostiles.

And for this sum of money, Travis Hooker and his rebel diehards would get their chance to whip into life the flames of a new rebellion.

Those men had not been idle, though, during the days the packet had been tied in at the Fort Lincoln landing. Hooker had schooled them well in the sly arts of sabotage and deadly attrition, teaching them how to do their work in the dark of night, Apache style.

There had been horses ridden out of Fort Lincoln that would go lame four or five days out, or die after eating poisoned grain. There had been wagon trains hauled out of Bismarck that would break down somewhere in those hostile hills out yonder, and the few teamsters who did manage to get through to their rendezvous with Canaday and McKinn would discover they had freighted medical supplies that had been corrupted beyond use and tainted rations that no trooper could force himself to eat.

That was not all. Two days after it happened, McCabe heard about the wagon outfit that had pulled out of Fort Lincoln carrying powder and small arms ammunition destined for Canaday's column. Long fuses had been rigged up in a way that only Travis

Hooker and Lou Savaine could have schemed. Nine Yankee teamsters and four escorting troopers had died in the explosions that destroyed the wagon train.

The officers sent out by General Sevier to investigate reported it an accident, a chain of explosions set off very probably by some teamster's careless match.

Travis Hooker, grinning at Branch McCabe, called it an act of guerrilla warfare that Charley Quantrill himself could not have pulled off any slicker.

As he measured his own position in this dark and deadly violence that was building up around him, the thought came again into McCabe's mind. *The step has been taken, and there's no turning back now.*

CHAPTER THIRTEEN

C LEE YANDELL SQUATTED on his heels outside the door of his engine room, listening to the soft rustling of the river currents along the hull of the packet. He wished to hell the time would come for the *Belle* to cast off. He didn't care where they went, up river or down, just so they got moving. It wore a man down, all this sitting and waiting, day in and day out. It gave him too much time to think about what he had come up the river to do, and sometimes he wondered if it was right or if he was crazy in the head for ever allowing the idea to take root.

Down-deck, near the racked cordwood, several roustabouts were hunkered down at a game of twenty-one. God-a'mighty, Yandell thought irritably, you'd think they'd get tired of bucking the same tiger all the time. He'd never cottoned much to anything but straight poker, which to his mind was the only game that gave a man a fair run for his money.

He turned his head to gaze once again toward the bow of the boat. Even in the dark of night, he could recognize Travis Hooker's lank shape, and he knew without doubt that the other two would be Lou Savaine and Logart. *Satan and his two shadows,* Clee Yandell thought sourly, and wondered what those three were cooking up against the Yankees this time.

They reminded Clee Yandell somehow of bratty kids sneaking out behind the outhouse to plot a new kind of devilment for the school teacher. Only those three weren't kids, but grown men. And it was never prankish devilment they hatched out, but mean and vicious trickery that only a renegade Apache could have prided himself in.

Like causing the mounts of that Yankee patrol to go lame, for instance, and poisoning their grain so that some of the animals would die. Like the kerosene that had been spilled over the bacon and beans in the wagon train that had pulled out of Bismarck four-five days ago, and calomel mixed into the flour. Seemed there was no bottom to the meanness that was in Travis Hooker, when it came to bluecoat troopers.

It was a hard thing for Clee Yandell to set straight in his mind. War was war, he tried to tell himself, and if you couldn't down your enemy with one weapon you grabbed up another.

But he had never had much stomach for this brand of fighting. He wondered what General Morgan would have said about that stunt Hooker and Savaine had pulled off, rigging that ammunition outfit up for an explosion, and thirteen men killed without ever knowing what hit them.

John Morgan would have used every word in the book, cussing out those three, given he wouldn't have ordered them lined up against a fence and shot. General Morgan had been that kind of a man, tough as a boot and as much a gentleman as a man could be when he was fighting a war.

Yandell had been on those raids behind the Yankee lines, and that strike through southern Indiana was one to remember. They had looted towns and farms along their way, and in two or three skirmishes with the Home Guardsmen they had fought grimly and killed. But always out in the open, and honorably. General Morgan's talents for war had never included Travis Hooker's brand of Apache murder.

Maybe times have changed, Yandell told himself, and what a man never done before he's got to do now if the South is ever going to whip the North in this new rebellion we came up here to start.

Lee Malvern came down from the cabin deck and sat down beside him, gazing toward the bow of the boat and the three men standing there.

"Wonder what they're up to this time?"

Yandell moved his shoulders irritably. "*¿Quién sabe?*"

Lee Malvern pulled his head around, scowling. "Now what is that supposed to mean?" he demanded.

"Spanish. Means 'who knows.' "

"Then why didn't you just out and say so?" Malvern snapped.

"Kind of crotchety, ain't you?"

"I'm tired of all this sittin' and waitin', is all. We came up here to fight Yankees, didn't we? Then why don't we get at it, I'd like to know?"

"Ask Hooker; he's the one running this show."

Malvern snorted. "All he does is pussy-foot around after dark. I never took to this Injun-style fighting."

Clee Yandell was in the grip of his own cranky dissatisfaction, and it fitted his mood to rawhide the crossness of the man with him.

"Didn't know you were such a fire-eater," he said. "What is your idea—that we grab up our guns and line out our sights against the bluecoats, us against Sevier's army?"

Malvern gave him a long smouldering look. "Are you telling me you're proud of the stunts Trav Hooker has been pulling off?" he demanded.

"I didn't say that."

"I'm getting so I can't stand the sight of my own goddamn face when I look in a mirror," Lee Malvern said savagely. "I'm not the only one, neither. Just about every other man in the outfit feels the same way about this kind of fighting."

Yandell spoke carefully. "Talking about pulling out, are they?"

"You know damn well they're not." Malvern's eyes were hot, bitter. "They'll stick, and they'll do their warring Hooker's way, if they have to. They won't like it, but they'll do it."

The mood that was in Clee Yandell was a dismal one. He rolled the cud of tobacco into his cheek, and spat down at the deck. "Maybe they'll like it better when McCabe comes up with the regiment of dead Yankees that he promised Hooker."

"You ask me, Branch McCabe is playing a sharp game all his own."

"He is," Yandell breathed, "he's a dead man the minute he tips his hand. It's something he knows, too. Me, I figure any Louisiana man who'd side with Yankees against his own people would sell his soul for the price of a bottle. McCabe's ante in this is ten thousand dollars, as I recollect."

"All right. So it's money he wants, and he doesn't care how he gets it," Malvern said savagely. "That regiment of dead Yankees— how are we going to pull that one off? Slip up on them at night while they're asleep and cut their throats?"

"It's how Charley Quantrill would have done."

"Quantrill was a goddamn murderer."

Clee Yandell stared off into the night. "Given time, my very good friend, maybe that is what we'll all be. You got any whisky, have you?"

"There's a bottle stashed away I know about."

"Let's you and me get drunk, Lee."

"You think that'll help any?"

"I keep thinking about what you said—about seeing yourself in a mirror. Maybe that's how I feel, too. We'll get drunk, friend, and then we'll bust every goddamn looking glass on this goddamn boat."

At midnight they made their way unsteadily into the combination saloon and dining room, picked up two chairs and sent them crashing into the great gold-framed mirror behind the bar.

To Clee Yandell and Lee Malvern it seemed like one hell of a good idea, at the time.

CHAPTER FOURTEEN

THERE WERE TIMES when Elise Casamore considered herself pitifully shallow and shamefully weak, when it seemed that the feeling she had discovered within herself for Branch McCabe would surely collapse under the weight of the terrible things it was demanding from her.

Loyalty, she had learned, could become an overwhelming burden when everything inside her wanted to forget the hurts and tragedies of the war. She had shed her share of tears, and now she wanted peace and her dreams for the future. But she realized that she could never have them, for in her mind and in her heart she had given herself to a man who had promised to deliver a regiment of Yankee troopers to their graves.

Each day she fought to bring into newer and sharper focus the hurts and injustices she had suffered during the rebellion, as if those wrongs might build a protective wall around her conscience. Her father and brother buried at Yellow Tavern, the memory of other relatives and friends killed on other fields; her mother dying not long after their home with its tall gables and beautiful white columns had been put to the torch by drunken Yankee rabble ... the hurts and bitterness in her were many.

She had every reason, she told herself, to hate the North and its people.

Yet she couldn't shut out of her mind the fact that there had undoubtedly been many Yankee women hurt just as cruelly by Southern raiders. Jo Shelby and John Morgan, among others, had carried the torch into the North many times, killing and plundering. Nor would she ever be able to forget the shocking stories she had heard about Quantrill's massacre of the town of Lawrence, of women brutally violated and every man and boy shot down on sight. Such cruel and vicious doings were enough to make the heart shudder.

And now it's starting all over again, she thought bitterly.

In later years, this remote landing on the upper Missouri would be known as the place where the second rebellion had been ignited. Only time could decide whether this place would become a memorial to rebel glory, or a monument to perfidy.

History would write many things about the *Southern Belle* and its crew. Renegades or patriots? Anarchists without conscience, or partisans of rare shining courage? The pages of books were not always colored by the honor of men, Elise knew.

She had heard enough whispering among her crew to know that Travis Hooker had not been idle during these days the *Belle* had been tied in at the landing. She knew about the lame and poisoned horses; she knew about the wagon-train explosions, and the thirteen dead Yankees.

A great melting wave of relief had rolled through Elise when she learned that Branch had not known about these acts until after they were done, and that most of her crew had not had a part in them.

Yet, behind this sense of relief was the fearsome knowledge that each day was bringing Branch closer to the promise he had made to Travis Hooker. It seemed beyond belief that Branch could be capable of such a thing. But she had heard his promise, and each word was like a flame standing raw-red and implacable in her mind. Each word was like a saber stabbed into the earth at the head of an open grave.

She knew she could not change him. A man like Branch McCabe was a rock no woman could ever move. She would have to accept him as he was, or put him out of her life.

Put Branch out of her life? What he had done during the war, the stand he had taken against the South, no longer mattered. She realized now that it had never really mattered, for she had loved him, it seemed, longer than she could remember. He was a part of every memory and every dream. And this, she knew, would always be so.

Whatever Branch was, she would have to learn to be. If he hated, she must also hate; if he sold his soul for money, then she must be willing to sell hers for the same price. The thought was like a cold blade twisting inside her heart. When a woman loved a man, she always stood beside him.

Only at night, when she was alone, was there any escape. There was a feeling of deep comfort, of a great and necessary release, in standing at the deck railing as she was now, letting her gaze reach out and beyond until it lost itself in the blackness of the night.

There was a sense of escape in looking up at the stars and then into the vast dark void beyond the stars, putting behind her for one small moment the world and all the tragedy that men brought to it with their violent ways.

But always Branch's promise to Travis Hooker came back to her, like echoes rushing down out of the black space above to crash through the caverns of her mind. And the night was a thousand eyes, staring down at her, damning her.

CHAPTER FIFTEEN

L OADED TO TWO HUNDRED TONS with medical and commissary supplies as well as small arms ammunition, the *Southern Belle* made her run up the lowering channels of the river.

At Fort Buford an escort company of sixty men commanded by Captain Stephen Baker came aboard to join Lieutenant Pryor and the courier who was to maintain liaison with General Turley's main force. McCabe at once pushed on, now pointing the packet up the Yellowstone toward the mouth of the Powder, where he was to rendezvous with Turley and General McKinn.

These were the long hard days when pressures built up in a man and turned his temper cross-grained and brittle, and each bend of the river held its own threat of danger.

Along this wild trace there were no wood yards. McCabe halted the packet at every deadfall or sizable thicket in order to keep his supply of fuel replenished. During these times a trooper stood watch on the texas deck, and scouts were sent out into the low greening hills to guard the wood cutters against a Sioux attack or ambush.

Dispatch riders picked up the boat as it thrust deeper into hostile country, bringing orders to McCabe and the latest information.

Major Rennig, scouting the country from the Powder to the Tongue with six troops of men and ten days' rations, sent word that he had found a heavy Indian trail along the Rosebud. Next day information reached the packet that General Canaday had run into a brief but violent battle in the hills some distance west of the Rosebud, but during the night had lost contact with the hostiles.

It became increasingly clear during those days of probing actions that the Sioux were massing to a strength never before known in the territory, and the gossip of hard-bitten troopers on the *Belle*'s decks changed from scornful confidence to a dark and moody foreboding.

A courier brought orders for McCabe to push on past the Tongue and tie in at the mouth of the Rosebud, where General McKinn was holding his troops. That night as he stood outside the pilot house, McCabe could see the campfires of McKinn's command burning redly against the darkness, and the voices of the rooks in that force were loud and boastful, trying to sound brave.

Near noon next day, he watched the long line of Colonel Maxwell Cady's proud Eleventh come trailing across the tableland and down into the valley of the Yellowstone. General Sevier was there waiting for him, and that night there was a council between the officers in Branch McCabe's cabin on the *Belle*.

The jaws of the trap were slowly and inexorably being closed on the Sioux. With his map spread out on McCabe's desk, Sevier traced the line of the Yellowstone with the bit of his pipe, giving his orders crisply to General McKinn.

"When you reach this point, I want you to swing south toward the forks of the Big and Little Horns."

It was this Hugh Sevier, McCabe recalled, who had made that storming drive through the shattered palisade and across the death-trap ditch of Fort Fisher, fighting his way over the traverses and through the casemates until the South's greatest earthwork fortress had fallen to the flag of the Federal forces.

"You should reach the forks on or about the 26th, at which time your scouts should be able to determine Colonel Cady's exact whereabouts. Do you understand?"

McKinn nodded. Sevier went on, laying out his plan of action in hard, concise tones. Cady was to move south along the

Rosebud to investigate the trail of the hostiles reported by Major Rennig. It would be a chancey maneuver.

Raising his eyes, Sevier spoke forcibly. "I can give you four troops of the Second, under Major Cathrow, if you want them."

There was a touch of rashness in Cady's sudden smile that brought back to McCabe's mind that whiplash attack across the torn fields at Yellow Tavern and Cedar Creek. Here was the man who had outfought Stuart and annihilated Early's command with his brash, rakehell tactics, and now that same note of cheerful audacity was in Cady's tone of voice.

"General, if I run into a Sioux force too big for my Eleventh, then it would also be too big for the Eleventh and those four troops you offer me."

Sevier frowned. "Then take along the three Gatling guns under Lieutenant Lowe. This could be a rough one, Max. You may need everything you can get out there."

Cady shook his head. His confidence was a shining, imperious thing. But if this was a weakness, Branch McCabe reflected, it was also the keystone of strength that was in all indomitable men. Forrest had had it, and Mosby and Stuart.

Sevier bent over the map again, then straightened to gaze at McCabe in sober concentration.

"I would like you to take your packet up the Little Big Horn as far as possible." He stood with both hands planted flat on the desk, like a man bracing himself against the dire consequences of any error he might make in this hard and dangerous campaign. "It's a risky thing I'm asking, Captain. But your boat is our base of supplies, and it's necessary that we have it as close as you can possibly get it to the headwaters of the Rosebud."

McCabe nodded. "I'll have it there."

The meeting was at an end, all decisions reached. McCabe stood alone in the room, remembering Sevier's final orders.

The *Southern Belle* had become the hub around which this great and deadly wheel was massively turning. In the holds of the packet were stores of rations and ammunition and medical supplies without which no army could survive on this hard and dangerous land.

His thoughts stumbled on, carrying him to the ultimate, the unescapable, for now he knew that the lives of a Yankee regiment had been consigned to the *Belle* and her rebel crew.

This, then, could be their harsh victory, and also their eternal shame....

CHAPTER SIXTEEN

THE DAY DAWNED clear and cool, with a steady wind sweeping out of the west. Buffalo could be seen grazing on the greening flanks of distant hills, and the swift currents of the Yellowstone ran in a clean bright glitter between the low islands. Against the high blue of the sky a scavenger bird traced its endless doom circles, making the minds of men turn to gray and fearsome thoughts.

The supplies for Cady's command were drawn from the packet's hold at dawn's first light, and along the bank of the river brown-faced men saw to their gear and readied their mounts, restless to be on the move.

It was a sight a man would remember. Horses snorting and blowing as cinch straps were yanked tight...the nervous recruit stepping behind a bush to water out for the second time within short minutes...steam rising from the droppings of pack mules...the cursing and ribald joshing of leathery-faced veterans, and above all this commotion the haranguing damnations of a bowleg sergeant who at any other time would have loudly boasted that his outfit was the bigod finest in any man's army.

The picture was always the same, Branch McCabe reflected as he watched from the packet's upper deck, for all fighting men, Yankees or Johnny Rebs, were hewn from the same sturdy stock.

He loaded his pipe and got it going, nagged by a strange restlessness, a fretting dissatisfaction. It was a queer thing, he thought. A man lived through a war and hated every minute of it. But when it was all behind him and he was off at one side watching other troopers make ready for battle, everything inside him turned quick and hot and almost envious.

But this wasn't envy in him, he knew, for he had had his fill of violence. He had smelled his share of gunsmoke, and had heard too many times the sickening sound of a bullet smashing home—the spurting redness and the voice of the stricken crying out to his God in agony.

No, it wasn't envy working on him, not that. It was pity for brave men riding out to die. And it was something more. It was his conscience telling him that this fight to tame a wild land was also his own.

Elise came up to the hurricane and joined him at the railing. Looking at her, he was shocked by the coldness of her eyes and the malice in the hard lines of her face as she watched the troopers form their lines on the river bank. Elise was the face of all the women he had seen along the dusty roads at Shiloh as victorious Yankees marched by, and McCabe spoke out quietly against it.

"All spit and vinegar, every one of them. But how many of them will be dead by the end of the week, I wonder?"

"Should that matter any to you?"

Her voice was like a wintry wind cutting deep into him. He did not reply.

Along the river bank shouts rang out, echoing and re-echoing off through the low hills. The formation was now taking shape as confusion jelled swiftly into disciplined order. Saddle leather creaked, and bit rings jingled in the crisp morning air. The troopers mounted. The column shaped out in a long line of twos, and then at command it took movement, passing in review before Sevier and McKinn.

Colonel Cady, sitting ramrod straight in his saddle, came back along that stern line of brown-faced men, the brim of his campaign hat cuffed back to a rakish angle, the morning wind tossing his long yellow hair and the flaring red tie he was wearing.

When he came to where Sevier and McKinn stood, he brought his mount around to a dancing halt, facing them with a flourish.

Sevier raised his hand in salute. "Luck, Max!"

General McKinn, in whom there were no vain pretenses at all, spoke forcibly. "Now, Cady, if you find the Sioux out there don't be greedy. Wait for me to join you."

The voices of those men reached clearly and distinctly to where McCabe and Elise stood, and it seemed to him there was a note of brash impatience in Cady's enigmatic reply.

"No, I will not."

Watching that long file of riders trail off into the low hills, Elise spoke with stinging scorn.

"It's not the Army's battle the great Maxwell Cady is fighting here. All that man is thinking about is finding the Sioux and winning some new glory for himself."

His pipe had gone out. McCabe scratched another match for it.

Gazing at Elise, he found himself remembering a time when Junius Brutus Booth and his son Edwin had come to New Orleans with a group of traveling dramatic actors. McCabe, a young boy then, had gone to the Opera House with his father and mother to witness the opening performance. Shortly before the first curtain, one of the players had been taken ill, and a local girl had been hastily recruited to take her place. McCabe had found himself watching this girl above all others as she struggled through her role in the drama, reading from the script because she didn't know the lines.

In some vague, obscure way, Elise reminded him of that girl. He didn't know why.

"The gallant Maxwell Cady! I've heard it said that several Cheyenne girls were taken captive three or four years ago when their village was destroyed by Cady's Eleventh. Cady kept one of them with him for the rest of the campaign. Singing Cloud was her name, and there was a child born to her that year—bastard son of the noble Colonel Cady!"

"That could be nothing more than barracks gossip, Elise."

"It is something I do not find the least bit difficult to believe about him," she flared back.

"He's a fighter. You've got to give him that much."

"A vain, self-centered glory hunter! A man who violated a captive Indian girl, and fathered a son he refuses to acknowledge!"

"No man is perfect," McCabe said. "None of us is pure."

He drew a slow breath, watching her soberly. She had always been beautiful, but now the beauty of this girl was like something chipped from ice, cold and inflexible, unyielding.

"You've changed, Elise."

"Me, Branch?"

He didn't try to explain. He felt very sorry for Elise Casamore, and a little sorry for himself. Just looking at her made him feel worn and drained out and miserably futile.

CHAPTER SEVENTEEN

THE DAWN WINDS had blown themselves out and now the air was still, as though standing off breathlessly on some high remote place to watch the grim and deadly duel being waged between Yankee columns and the elusive Sioux.

Lordy, but this was about the hugest land a man could ever expect to see, Jubal told himself, with the far-away hills so cleanly etched against the sky that the mind couldn't get a fair grip on the distance between. When he stepped back from the firebox and had a look around, the vastness and immensity of the land seemed to come rushing at him and smash full upon him in a way that made him feel like an ant crawling across a plain that was without limit or end.

Jubal nosed the still air, drawing it into his lungs, then letting go of it slowly. It was starting to get hot, now that the sun was halfway up to noon.

Like as not, Melinda would put it down that he was only yarning if he told her about the days turning off so hot after nights that fairly chilled a man to his bones. It wasn't like this in Memphis, where he and Melinda had settled after the shooting was over. In Memphis, a man and his woman could sleep raw as jaybirds of a night, given they didn't have young'ns around to see more than was fittin' for innocent eyes.

Jubal stood back from the glowing firebox and looked away across the plains, toward the distant hills where Colonel Max Cady's column had gone in search of the Sioux.

The thought kept coming back into his mind: how did Cap'n McCabe plan to deliver that regiment of bluecoats to their graves, like he promised Travis Hooker?

He had heard gossip among the packet's crew and roustabouts. They would get their chance at the Yankees after the Sioux had hacked them down to size. Or they would slip something into their commissary supplies to make them sick, then wipe them out before they could get organized enough to fight back. The speculation changed from hour to hour. Or they would bury kegs of fused gunpowder where the troopers would bed down, and set them off after dark when the Yankees were asleep.

Such doings did not set well in Jubal's mind. They sounded more like the schemings of white trash like Travis Hooker and Lou Savaine than of a quality man like Cap'n Branch McCabe.

A thought told Jubal that there were not many men in the crew who would cotton to shooting down sick troopers, or setting off gunpowder at night while they were asleep. War was war and winning was the thing, Jubal allowed, but there was something dishonest and snake-mean about that kind of killing that would put ghosts in a man's mind for the rest of his life.

But he reckoned he and the crew would go along with this Quantrill-style warring if that was what Cap'n McCabe wanted. Wasn't for them to say what was right and what was wrong. Man had to do what he was told, when he was mixed up in a trouble this big, and try to make peace with his conscience after the fighting was over. But, Jubal wondered, could a man ever get away from the ghosts of the dead ones?

Lee Malvern came trotting up the passageway. "We've got some fast water up ahead. Yandell will need more steam."

"Yassah."

"Something eating on you, Jubal?"

"I ain't never killed a man afore," Jubal answered. "Time comes I got to, I reckon I could prob'bly do it easier a-mind if I knowed it was an honest fight."

Malvern frowned. "What are you talking about, man?"

"I just don't want to feel like a murderer afterwards," Jubal said. "I purely don't, Mistah Malvern, no matter what the Yankees ever done."

Well, we've left McKinn's column way back there behind us, Branch McCabe thought. *From here on, we're going to be on our lonesome.*

He was caught up suddenly by something harsh and fearsome in that thought. It was as though a huge and implacable menace, long dreaded from a distance, had all at once taken shape close in front of him, even more terrible in reality than it had been in his mind.

He knew now that he shouldn't have taken the gamble, that the risk was far greater than any one man had a right to take upon himself. It didn't help any to be able to say that what he'd done he'd had to do. One way or another, with his help or without it, Travis Hooker and the packet's rebel crew meant to have what they had come up the river to get.

One small shadow of hope clung to Branch McCabe: talk was often easier than the doing. And there were times when a man could not swallow what he had set his teeth to.

When he made the swing into the mouth of the Big Horn, the packet was confronted almost immediately by a rapids she could not defeat with her wheels alone. McCabe put a crew of roustabouts and escort troopers ashore, and sent them up the bank with a long warping cable to anchor around a tree. With the capstans in motion, reeling in the line, the *Belle* dragged herself up through the rapids to less violent waters.

They forced on, tying in at an island at night, and moving out again at dawn's first light. It was the toughest kind of steamboating, for never before had these waters been traveled by such a craft.

The going was slow, tedious. They nooned at the edge of bare hills, and tied in again when night closed around them. Throughout those long hard days, they fought their way up twisting channels, past overhanging cutbanks and through a gnarled and naked badlands, each bend of the river holding its own threat of snags and sandbars, or a Sioux ambush.

McCabe's map had soon proved to be entirely inaccurate, giving him only the sketchiest picture of this wild land he was invading. When the hills opened out again, he searched the far slopes for signs of a dispatch rider from Turley or McKinn. But none came. The land was vast and still, concealing a thousand dangers behind its tawny hills. The question kept nagging McCabe's mind: *Where the hell is Turley's dispatch rider?*

Each mile was carrying the packet into shallower waters, adding to the dangers of running aground or hitting a sawyer. Gravel bars pinched the main channel in with ever increasing frequency, and there were times when McCabe had the ridiculous impression of piloting the steamboat across bare land. But he found nothing amusing in the impression. *A horse could piddle more than I've got under me most of the time,* he thought bitterly.

He had no idea at all now of McKinn's position, and by sheer guesswork calculated that Turley's column should be somewhere in the hills far to the east as shown on the map somewhere in the vicinity of Turlock's Fork. Of Colonel Cady's command he had no idea at all, for he knew that officer to be one who made his decisions while on the field, boldly and sometimes impetuously, but always with a fine disregard for rules and regulations.

When the packet at last reached a point where the channel was less than three feet deep, McCabe refused to risk trying to push on any farther. He tied in at a low grassy bank. Hap Burwell and Kennerly stood watch on the texas deck while Captain Baker positioned his troopers along the banks to guard against an attack.

The day was hot, the air still and empty. A coyote drifted through the brush on a hill slope in the distance like a gray shadow.

A hell of a thing if the Sioux catch us here, McCabe thought.

Travis Hooker stood at the forward railing of the cabin deck, waiting for Logart and Lou Savaine to finish their circuit of the boat and join him.

This could be the time to do it, a thought told him, and he felt everything go quick and tight inside him, the same as when he had measured out that last gaunt minute outside the Kansas town, waiting for Charley Quantrill to give his signal to tilt the black flag forward for the attack.

There had been a man to ride with, Quantrill—cagey as a swamp fox, and hard as a Spanish spur. None of those highfalutin ideas in Charley Quantrill as tangled up the thinking and doing of most other officers fighting a war. The others could have their goddamn code of conduct, but Quantrill had done his fighting according to his own rules. Of which they had been few and seldom, Travis Hooker remembered, and smiled thinly to himself.

A few more officers like Charley Quantrill, and the South would never have been hacked down to its knees, with carpetbaggers swarming in afterwards like maggots feasting on a gut-shot body and Northern politicians and Union Leaguers strutting the streets of Memphis and New Orleans, passing laws intended only to put money in their own pockets and make the South beg for crumbs.

A few more fighters like Charley Quantrill, and it would have been the goddamn Yankees doing the crawling. Hooker spat across the railing, down at the river. Quantrill had known how to do it. Like when he hit that town of Lawrence, shooting down every Jayhawker man and boy on sight, and letting his men have themselves a time with the women before looting the place and putting the torch to it.

Travis Hooker's thoughts reached out and on. Given a little more luck, Quantrill would have carried through with his plan to fill Abe Lincoln full of lead, after Lee had handed the South over at Appomattox. That goddamn scrap of paper hadn't ended the war for Charley Quantrill and his black flag raiders. He had outfitted his men in stolen Federal uniforms and set out for Washington, with his gun loaded up for Abe Lincoln.

He would have emptied it into Lincoln, too, given some nigger-loving turncoats in Kentucky hadn't recognized him and tipped off the Federals. Now Quantrill was dead and in his grave, and a handful of men who had ridden under him were picking up the fight.

Hooker studied the positions of the escort troopers deployed along the banks of the river. The conviction kept growing in his mind, hard-edged and grainy. Now could be the right time to hit them, while they were watching the hills for the Sioux.

Logart and Lou Savaine came along the promenade and joined him at the railing. Logart chewed the end from a cable twist of tobacco, rolled it into one cheek, and slowly grinned.

"Looks as how they've done all they could to make it easy for us."

Hooker swung his attention to Lou Savaine.

"There's that Gatling gun set up on the main deck," Savaine said. "Given we can take it first off, the rest will be a breeze."

"How long will you need to get the rest of the crew ready?"

"Ten minutes, maybe fifteen. Wouldn't want to hurry it too much, though. Strikes me them bluecoats are a mite leery of some of us."

It was the one thing that bothered Travis Hooker. More than one of his rebel hotheads had not found it easy to hide their hatred for Yankee troopers.

"What about McCabe?" Lou Savaine asked.

"You get our boys ready," Hooker answered. "McCabe is the one to take over that Gatling gun for us."

Logart was doubtful. "You figure he'll do it?"

Travis Hooker nodded meagerly. "He'll do it, all right," he said.

Stepping out of her cabin, Elise Casamore saw Hooker cross the deck and start up the stairs toward the pilot house. One look at his face told her all she needed to know. The time had come. The blow was to be struck today, now.

She turned and went up the stairs behind Hooker, following him. A single thought cried out in her mind, a silent prayer: *Dear God, give me the strength to be the kind of woman Branch will need in this terrible thing he is about to do!*

CHAPTER EIGHTEEN

"**I**'VE COME AFTER that regiment of Yankees you said you'd give us," Travis Hooker said, and his gaze was bleak and mocking through the smoke of his thin black cheroot.

Branch McCabe stood with the great spoked wheel at his back. In his mind was the wish, gray and dismal, that he could turn around and fasten his big hands on the wheel, and steer the packet away from this thing that had now come against him.

But there was no way out, no escape. *I waited too long,* he thought emptily. Or maybe he had not been permitted to wait long enough. Too early or too late, there was no sure answer for a thing like this. The time was now, and there was no way around it.

"There are fifty, maybe sixty troopers in the escort Turley gave us," he said. "I wouldn't call that a Yankee regiment."

"They'll do for a starter," Hooker answered. "The rest we'll collect in due time."

There was something hard and jarring beneath the surface of the man's soft laughter, like the gritty edge of cold granite felt beneath black velvet.

"We'll collect your regiment, and then some. Run out on Turley now, and he's stranded way to hell and gone out here in the middle of nowhere, short of rations and ammunition and with the Sioux chewing on him from all sides. Let's hear you come up with a better idea for knocking a Yankee army apart."

"Some of them would get back," McCabe said.

"I'll trade them that would for them that won't."

Elise had followed Hooker into the wheelhouse. McCabe looked at her.

"What do you think about this?" he asked her.

Her eyes were unreadable, her face a loveliness carved from cold stone. "I want what you want, Branch. Nothing more, nothing less."

"The same as Hooker wants, Elise?"

"Is there any difference?" she asked, her voice as flat, as toneless as a man's.

He brought his gaze back to Hooker, pointing toward the troopers along the river bank. "They outnumber you three to one."

"One round of shots," Hooker said, "and the odds are only two to one. I've got men with me who have tied into worse odds than that before and come out on top."

McCabe drew a breath. "You've got it all figured out, haven't you?"

"Right down to the nails in Yankee coffins, McCabe. All I want from you is that Gatling gun they've set up down on the main deck. Once we get that, we're in. There never was a better equalizer than a Gatling. It can chew down the rest of those bluecoats before they know what's going off. Your job is to get that gun for us."

McCabe had one more look at the girl. Her face was taut, all expression sealed out; her eyes were the cold, implacable blue of a winter sky. Nothing he could say would reach her. He couldn't touch her. She seemed remote and far away, and there was no way that he could get to her.

"All right," he said. "All right."

Elise turned, swiftly and suddenly, and went out of the room.

Travis Hooker glanced at his watch, then raised his hard eyes to McCabe. "Eleven o'clock sharp is your time to do it," he said, and laughter rustled low in his throat. "That will put our Yankee friends in hell right on time for their noon meals."

CHAPTER NINETEEN

I T WAS FIVE until eleven.

Moving past the long racks of cut wood, Branch McCabe made his way toward the bow of the main deck, where the Gatling gun had been set up. A sergeant and two leathery-faced troopers were standing near the gun, scanning the hills around. *They can be handled,* he thought narrowly. The two troopers did not have enough heft to make much trouble, and the sergeant would not have much time to act. The element of surprise was the most potent of weapons at a time like this.

He paused beside one of the capstans, knowing he had to measure the minutes out carefully. Too soon would be an unforgivable mistake, and too late could be fatal. Travis Hooker was not a man to accept anything but perfection.

He was aware of Elise watching him from the deck above. How much did he owe this girl? The question sank deep into his mind; it echoed against his conscience. He could not find the answer.

He thought of the packet's crew, and of the cruel marks left on them and the South by a futile war. Appomattox had not erased all the malice. Many of the victors were harsh and pitiless in the retribution they demanded from the defeated, and not enough time had passed for forgiveness.

The *Belle*'s crew and roustabouts still hated. They were diehards who had never stopped fighting, who had come up a long river to carry a new and more relentless war to the North.

They were not alone. The James boys and the Youngers still raided and plundered. And there was Jo Shelby, who had lowered

his tattered but unconquered battle flag into the muddy currents of the Rio Grande, and then with five hundred of his Iron
Brigade had marched across the river into Mexico, defiant in his
refusal to surrender, and vowing that the day would come when
he would return to strike newer and greater blows at the North.

This could be that day, Branch McCabe thought moodily.

The time had come, the last lean seconds measured off.
McCabe stepped forward. He moved steadily, unhurriedly, as a
man should move when he plays the sharp and brutal game of
unwarned violence.

He saw the sergeant face around in his direction, casually
curious. He saw the thick coil of rope on the deck just short of
the man.

As he moved closer, he was aware of sharp and glittering
images etched into his consciousness—of Elise watching...of
Lou Savaine and Logart and Travis Hooker and all those other
hard-faced men waiting for him to make the move that would
unleash the furies that were in them.

He knew he was expected to divert the attention of the three
troopers, and as he moved closer he glanced past them, toward
the hills.

Through that weight of silence, he spoke. "Sergeant, I think it
would be wise if you sent a few men ... "

His foot struck the coil of rope, and he stumbled. As he
pitched forward, he saw the sergeant's hands grab out to break
his fall, but the weight of his momentum was too much for them,
and he slammed headlong against the wheel of the gun carriage.

Through the sudden burst of pain that exploded between his
temples, he heard the sergeant's hard shout. "Give me a hand,
somebody! This man has been hurt."

Elise watched silently as Lee Malvern and Jubal cleansed the
deep gash in McCabe's scalp, and fashioned a crude bandage
for it. During these minutes in Branch's cabin, Travis Hooker

had cursed with rabid fury as he savagely paced back and forth across the small room. Now he heeled sharply around to glare at McCabe with hot and hating eyes.

"We had it all set up," he said harshly. "We were all ready to start knocking over those blue-bellies the instant you got your hands on that Gatling gun. Then you had to stumble over that coil of rope, bash your goddamn head in, and blow the whole play. You ought to be gut-shot, McCabe, and if I thought this was anything but an accident I'd do just that, right here and now!"

Lee Malvern looked at Jubal. They straightened, watching Travis Hooker soberly.

"There'll be another time," McCabe said. He looked at Elise for a moment. "A better time and a better way, Hooker—and soon."

Elise turned abruptly, and went out of the room.

For one brief space of time she had imagined that what Branch had done was not an accident, that tripping over the coil of rope had been something grimly and desperately intentional.

But now she knew that this was not so. His voice, his eyes and the stony lines of his face had told her that this was not so.

CHAPTER TWENTY

THEY SAW IT FIRST as a thickening haze, a dingy discoloration suspended above the far horizon; within minutes it became dark columns of heavy smoke rolling up from the distant hills. Where the upper winds caught it, the smoke flattened out and stretched like a tattered banner across the pale blue of the sky. It was too far away for sound to carry.

One trooper announced without much conviction that it marked the location of a big Sioux village that had been put to the torch. But the man next to him did not agree, voicing the opinion that the smoke was that of battle, and God help the troopers who were fighting it.

The afternoon faded. Night closed in on the packet, each passing hour bringing its own nagging fears. At dawn, Captain Baker's scouts came drifting back from their long vigil in the hills, tired and disgruntled, and with no news to report. The troopers deployed along the river banks rose up from the cold ground to stretch aching muscles and knuckle red-rimmed eyes, cursing the new day with the grainy virulence of men tired to the bone and pestered by more worries than the mind could name.

It was this waiting and wondering, Branch McCabe knew, that could erode the nerves until the raging violence of battle would come as a great and blessed relief. He paced the deck in the gray light of dawn, the mutterings of the troopers raising old and familiar echoes through his memory.

"Man's a plain idiot to let himself in for a life like this. Freeze all night and sweat all day, and the rations they hand you a coyote wouldn't eat. You got a smoke on you, Lafe?"

"John Jacob Astor, millionaire, that's me! Why don't you buy your own, for a change?"

"I'm saving up my money to buy fleas for a dog. I got a million of my own right now, but they're all like brothers to me. Got a match, have you?"

"Godamighty! Next thing I know, you'll be wanting to borry my straddle, next time you go out with a woman!"

"I got fixin's of my own that I never get a chance to use. You figure the Sioux know we're here, Lafe?"

"Man can't scratch himself out here without the Sioux knowing it afore he's finished. They've got us spotted all right. Like as not, they'll lose Cady and Rennig back there in the hills, and come down on us like a runaway wagon."

"That was a big smoke off there yesterday. If it was a fight, it must have been a bitch."

"It's this goddamn waiting that chews a man down. You ever been scared, have you?"

"If I had an extry pair, I'd be changing my drawers right now. Let's have another match, Lafe. That tobacco of yours burns like stable scrapings."

"That's just what it is, Mister Monahan. I had you in mind when the mule dropped it."

The mists lifted from the river, for a brief while hanging above the bottomlands like thin tendrils of smoke. The sun lifted from behind the far hills, reaching into the sky. A wind came out of the north in short, fitful gusts, and then the air turned still again. The mists were gone, leaving the land etched in crystal clarity.

McCabe looked to the east. The heavy columns of smoke were no longer to be seen above the distant hills. The land all around lay silent and empty.

Captain Baker sent his scouts out again, and ordered his troopers to hold their positions along the river bank. Sam Carthage and Tully Kennerly walked past, their abrasive voices reaching across to where McCabe stood.

"There's enough Sioux out there in them hills to put us under in no time at all, given they take the notion."

"Might not be quite that easy, is my idea," Tully Kennerly said. "Takes a lot of biting to chew up sixty bluecoats who are ready and waiting."

"It's a chore I'd think twice before taking on, for a fact."

"You were all set to take a whack at them yesterday, as I recollect."

"That's the trouble with you," said Sam Carthage sourly. "You talk too damned much."

Mid-morning, one of Baker's scouts crested a high point of land a thousand yards distant, gesturing wildly and pointing off to the southeast. Sergeant Geary shouted his whiplash command, and the Gatling gun at the packet's bow swung around in that direction. Along the river bank there sounded the metallic clatter of loads ramming home, and on the decks of the *Belle* the voices of men turned thin and sharp.

The land out there lay silent, green-gray and empty. Then out of the emptiness an Indian suddenly appeared, racing his winded pony down the creased flanks of the hill and through the willow thickets toward the packet.

A wild-eyed trooper, his nerves suddenly letting go, shouted and yanked his rifle to shoulder; down the line another man yelled stridently at him.

"Hold it, you! He ain't no blanket Indian!"

The silence clamped down again. It was a crushing thing. Except for the lone Indian racing toward the packet, the hills around remained still and empty. But that in itself was enough to tighten the guard of a knowing man: the time to be afraid of a Sioux was when you couldn't see him.

Movement nearby brought McCabe's attention snapping around. It was Elise coming across the deck toward him.

He said harshly, "Get back to your cabin."

She shook her head, her eyes following the onrushing rider.

"For God's sake, Elise!"

"I think I've seen that rider before, Branch."

McCabe heeled sharply around. The rider was hauling his sweating mount to a halt at the shallows of the river. Naked but for a breechclout, the Indian lifted his carbine aloft in the sign of peace. Recognition hit Branch McCabe then. This Indian was one of the scouts who had ridden off with Cady's column.

And recognition brought a hard oath from one of the troopers on the deck below. "He's that Crow scout who always rode with Charley Lowe. The one they call Curly! Mother of God, something has happened to the Eleventh!"

The Indian came on, riding through the shallows to the packet, still holding his carbine high and shaking his head. He slid down from the horse, into the water. Hands reached out and hauled him onto the boat.

Watching from above, McCabe saw the scout hand his rifle to one of the troopers. Then an expression of tragedy and grief broke across his square dark features, and he began making gestures with his hands, all the time shaking his head and groaning and crying out in the tongue of the Crows.

Captain Baker was down there. He swung around, a hard urgency in his voice. "Does anyone here know Crow?" None did. He swore bitterly. "He's trying to tell us what happened, but there's no way for him to get it across."

One of the roustabouts called out. "Maybe he could do it with picture talk, Cap'n."

It was a chance, one small hope for opening the door between two alien tongues. Baker brought out a pencil and paper, and showed the Indian how to use them. The pencil clamped in his fist, the Crow squatted on the deck and began drawing crude lines. He drew two circles, one inside the other, and in the space between he made many small marks, identifying them in a voice of unmistakable despair.

"Sioux! Sioux!"

Then he filled the inner circle with similar crude markings, and now the Indian's voice took on the low wailing of grief.

"*Absaroka!*" He said it again and again. "*Absaroka!*"

Now a trooper spoke out with sudden comprehension. "By God, that much Crow I savvy! It means great warriors—soldiers—something like that. He's talking about the Eleventh. Almighty God, he's telling us Cady was caught in a trap by the Sioux!"

The Indian dropped the pencil and stood up. His face twisted with pain and anguish as he struck his chest again and again with a clenched fist, gestures that no man who had fought in the violence of battle could ever fail to comprehend.

"Boom, boom! *Absaroka!* Boom, boom, boom!"

He clutched his scalp lock with one hand, and with the other raked a tight circle around it, as with a knife. He made a motion as though to yank the scalp off and tie it to his belt, all the while imitating the war dance of the Sioux. Then he bent as if over the body of a fallen man, and with his knife indicated the vicious slashing of the Sioux death mark—a gash slit from knee to hip, bone deep.

Of such things there was no need for words. A wrenching sickness dug deep and cold into Branch McCabe as he looked on, and the scene painted by this Crow scout was etched stark and terrible in the minds of all those watching. They saw the Sioux massing their savagery around the encircled Eleventh, and in their minds they heard the shrieking war cries of the hostiles and the thunder of gunfire, and in the depths of their souls they witnessed the final valiant stand of Cady's shattered ranks.

The Crow was silent. There was no more. It was told.

This, then, was the massacre of Cady and his proud Eleventh.

McCabe looked around at Elise, and saw the horror that was in her eyes. He looked at Carthage, Malvern and Clee Yandell, at Hap Burwell and Tully Kennerly, and the giant Negro, Jubal. They were men looking into themselves, and seeing pity and regret for those who had died.

But not Travis Hooker, who was softly laughing. Nor Logart and Lou Savaine. Death was what they had come up the river to give to men like Colonel Maxwell Cady and his Eleventh. It made no difference that it was the Sioux who had done the killing. One way, to them, was as good as another.

Captain Baker lifted his gaze to the deck above, to McCabe. "All we can do now is wait," he said.

CHAPTER TWENTY-ONE

H IS NAME WAS Muggins Taylor, and he came riding out of the dusk on a roan mare that had been all but killed by the miles it had covered that day.

Stringy, saddle-warped, with a face weathered by wind and sun to the color of old cavalry leather, he came out of the long shadows, out of the hard wild hills where death was a thousand painted faces and a thousand daubed bodies massed on the land to crush and destroy.

Muggins Taylor, the name of a man who would be forever haunted by the savagery he had witnessed. He was talking with the troopers on the packet.

"I was trying to get through to Fort Ellis with some dispatches from General McKinn when the Sioux cut my trail. I've been dodging them since before sun-up yesterday. It was close, close. This boat hadn't been here, I wouldn't be either, by now, way they were getting me boxed. A man never knows how bigod close he is to his grave."

His voice was a nerve-edged rasp as he tried to talk the pressures out of himself. He couldn't force himself to eat. He was tired and beaten and the torments of all the brutal miles he had traveled were still in him, and all he wanted to do was talk. Someone handed him a cheroot and he continued.

"I was attached to Turley's outfit when we got to the place where the Eleventh caught it. That was two, three days ago, I think. Maybe more. Hell, I don't know. All I remember is what we found on that damn hill. Dead. All of them dead. Sturgick and Myles. Cady and his brother, and Audey Reese. That newspaper writer, too—what was his name?"

"Mark Purcell?" McCabe asked.

"Yeah, him. Mark Purcell, shot through the head, and his portfolio still on the ground beside him. Dead horses and pack mules, and all the men slit to the bone from hip to knee with the Sioux death mark. If I live to be a hundred … if I live to be a hundred years old, I won't never forget …" He stopped talking, staring off into space.

He turned his head after a while, blinking his eyes at one of the troopers crowding around. "That you, Emmett?" he asked.

"It's me, boy."

"Must be something in my eyes," Muggins Taylor said. "I can't see so well, some reason." He drew a long ragged breath, still looking at Emmett. "You recollect Hank Wyman, do you?" he asked.

"I remember him."

"The one as used to like his monte games so well every time he got his pay? Short, easy-goin' feller … "

"I remember him," Emmett said again.

"He's dead."

"God rest his soul."

"Emmett, if I live to be a hundred years old … "

"Stop talking about it, friend. Try not to think about it any more."

"Hank never was worth shucks at monte," Muggins kept on. "He always lost more than he ever won. Funny how a man like Hank will stick to a game he's no good at."

Emmett said nothing. He took the cheroot from the trooper's hand, got it going, then put it between the tight gray lips.

That moment Muggins Taylor was looking past the decks of the packet, past the banks of the Little Big Horn, out past the dimming hills.

"Hank Wyman. Soldiered with him at Cedar Creek and Pittsburg Landing. I owed him nine dollars. A short, easy-going feller. Then I found him on that goddamn hill with a Sioux lance busted off in him. Looking up at the sky, he was, just looking up at the sky … "

"A drink, Muggins?"

"I couldn't hold one down."

"What about the others—Turley and McKinn?"

"I don't know. Since I seen them last, I just don't know. Every Sioux ever born is out there in them hills." He shook his head. "Did I tell you about Colonel Cady's kid brother getting it? Young Ben Cady?"

"You told us," Emmett said.

"Him and Audey Reese, both," Taylor said.

"What about Rennig's command?"

"Who?"

"Major Rennig," Emmett repeated.

"They hit him, too. Cut him off and held him pinned down so he couldn't get to the Eleventh."

"Christ!"

"Did I tell you about Rennig's wounded?" Muggins Taylor wanted to know, a part of his mind still on the far-away hills.

"Keep talking," Emmett said, sharper now.

"They're trying to get through to here—thirty, maybe forty of the worst hit, on mule litters. Two troops of the Second are with them, but they won't stand a prayer of making it if the Sioux pick up their trail. They don't show up tonight, I reckon they won't never, God pity their souls."

The last light of day was given to clearing the after section of the main deck, and covering the planks with grass cuttings to form an immense padding for the wounded. When the medicine chests were arranged close around for ready use, there was nothing more that could be done.

Night closed in. A string of fires were ignited along the trail to guide the ambulance detail in to the packet, but only luck could carry them through the wild hills out yonder.

The packet creaked against her shore lines, waiting out the hours in silence. Troopers patrolled the river banks and the rim of the hills, walking in lonely fear.

They came out of the blackness of night, with battle-etched troopers of the Second guarding the flanks of the slow-moving column. They were a long string of mules stretching away into the darkness, each dragging a travois made of lodgepoles taken from an abandoned Sioux camp, with tent canvas stretched between to form a crude litter for the wounded.

Branch McCabe stood at the packet's lowered staging as the wounded were carried on board. Elise was beside him, seeing the drawn gray faces and the shock-dulled eyes of men struck down by the savagery of the Sioux.

The *Belle*'s rebel crew was there, men who had seen the agony of gunshots and slashing blades on other battlefields and knew the bitter flavor of it.

And yonder was Logart, Lou Savaine, Travis Hooker. Men who gazed at each wounded trooper with the pitiless malice of the unforgiving.

When the last of them had been carried past, McCabe looked at the girl beside him.

"Alive or dead," he said, "they belong to the *Belle* now."

He turned and walked away from her. He went up the stairs and into his cabin. He didn't light the lamp. He pulled off his boots and stretched out on the bunk, gazing up through the darkness at the images it brought to his mind.

The battle-etched faces of the Second, unwashed and weary...

The dullness of shock in the eyes of the stricken...

The gentleness of the hard-bitten troopers who had carried the wounded aboard...

That night Branch McCabe slept the sleep of the damned.

CHAPTER TWENTY-TWO

J ubal...

Long as I live, I won't never forget it. One minute them hills was empty as an owned darky's pockets, and the next minute the Injuns came spillin' across the ridges and out'n the valleys, riding hard and wild and kicking up such a sight of dust that them behind couldn't hardly be seen.

Lawse, but it was a fearsome thing, first look, all them feathered bonnets and daubed faces and painted ponies a-comin' down at the packet faster almost than a man can think.

But it was kind of handsome, too, know what I mean. It was something a man cain't put into plain words. Handsome in a wild kind of way, like when the sky colors up red and purple and greenish just afore a storm, with lightning jabbing and thunder pounding closer and closer. Handsome like that, wild and scarey.

I like to jumped out of my shoes when Marse Yandell shoved a rifle in my hand and yelled at me to start using it. He said they were after my scalp, too.

That hit me as kind of funny, first off, the notion of any Sioux wanting to take my scalp, hair short and kinky as mine. Then all of a sudden I recollected seeing a man once after his scalp had been tooken, the skin of his face sagging down loose as dewlaps, and awful to look at. And all at once I got it in my head that them injuns rushing down at us, yelling and shooting, was God-awful real, and if they did what they aimed to do I wouldn't be around much longer to look after Melinda and our young'uns.

Guns were going off all around me on the packet and where the bluecoats were dug in along the river bank, but for some reason the shots seemed dull and far off. A little ways down the deck from me a man of a sudden started threshing around and screaming something fierce. I didn't know who he was, Yankee or Johnny Reb. But I knowed it might've been me instead of him, bullet-hit.

I got down on one knee and pointed the rifle, not at any particular Injun but at the whole mess of them, dazed like. I yanked the trigger, but nothing happened. I felt real foolish when I got it into my head that I'd forgot to cock the hammer. It was the first time I was ever in a shooting fight.

I thumbed back the hammer, and pulled the trigger again. All I hit was the sky. The carbine like to jumped out'n my hands, it being a big-bore shooter and me used to that old squirrel rifle I had back in Louis'ana.

But the racket it made and the way it smacked back against my shoulder sort of steadied me down. After that I lined up the sights close as I could when about all you could see to shoot at on them running ponies was an arm and leg and daubed face under the animal's neck.

Wouldn't have been much to stop the Sioux that day if'n it wasn't for the bluecoats. It was a glory to watch them hunkered down steady and cool-like, with more Sioux than a man could count rushing down the hill at them like a painted cloud. I reckon all the *Belle*'s crew and roustabouts were busy too, but it was the Yankees that was out there on the bank to take the worst jolt.

None of them as I could see ever got rattled though, even when it looked like they was going to get rode over. They didn't waste many shots, them bluecoats. When they couldn't line up on a man, they shot down his pony and dropped the warrior after.

I kept cocking and pulling the trigger a long time after my gun was empty, too scared in my head to know what I was doing, clear. I had to hunt up Marse Yandell to get more shells, and by then the Sioux had cut back out of shooting range to get ready to rush us again.

It was the Yankees that pulled their stopper, that first rush. They're all men, by glory.

Clee Yandell...

Just look at them, out there. All paint and feathers and howling hell. That first time in I thought they had us, for sure.

They only knew it, they could have rubbed us out that first rush. Wasn't a dozen men on this boat that wasn't unloaded, then. But not those Yankees, by God. They had enough sense to save a few rounds for the right time, and they had the guts to hold steady and make each shot count. That's what broke up that first rush, and sent the Sioux high-tailing it back there for more medicine.

Look at that medicine man prance around. Sounds like a peacock, him and his goddamn yammering. Looks like one too, all paint and feathers, except for them buffalo horns sticking out of his head.

You'd better blow up your biggest wind ever, my fine feathered friend. You've got enough warriors behind you to pull off this job, but I'm here to say a mess of you will be singing out of the other side of your mouth before you put the last of these Yankees under. They know a bigod thing or two about fighting, they do. They whupped us rebels, didn't they, and it takes about the best there is to do that.

Tully Kennerly...

Our Father which art in heaven, hallowed be Thy name...

Logart...

Come on, you paint-smeared bastards. Kill off these Yankees for us, and you're welcome to any rebel scalps you can take.

Travis Hooker...

How many times are they going to let these bluecoats throw them back? There must be three or four hundred of them out there, and most of them are using guns taken from the Eleventh, sounds like to me. If they could finish off that fancy-pants Colonel Cady, they ought to be able to put these Yankees under.

Come on, then; come on, damn you! Form your lines, head out, and don't stop until you've got what you want. That's how Charley Quantrill used to do it, and he put more blue-bellies in their graves than will ever be counted. Quantrill would have made one rush, and that'd been it. But this is your third try now, and you haven't cut the mustard yet.

It's that goddamn Gatling gun. It chews down their front line so fast that those behind lose their sand. All right then, I'll take care of that Gatling gun for you, and once you've finished off these Yankees I'll make you a deal that will give you all the guns you'll ever want, you and all the other tribes. A little help from you Sioux, and there'll be a rebel army marching into Washington before much longer to make the Yankees eat some of the crow they've been feeding to the South.

That Gatling gun. That blue uniform you're wearing makes a mighty fine target, Sergeant—right between the shoulder blades!

Sergeant Geary…

I thought of you again last night, Mary. I guess I haven't written to you often enough of late, but if we pull through this fight I promise… God! *Dear God in heaven* ….

Branch McCabe…

Well, here they come again. Last time I thought they were going to snow under those Yankees out there on the bank, but they just couldn't take what it cost.

Funny about Indians. Most times they go into a war like it was a kind of a game. They fight like fury, but like as not right when they're at the point of winning some fool thing happens that makes them decide their medicine is bad, and they turn tail.

But it won't be like that today, I guess. These devils are part of the bunch that cut down the Eleventh. Their medicine is big, and they aim to add our scalps to their collection. Would have done it before now, too, hadn't been for that Gatling gun down there on the main deck.

How come they're holding back with the Gatling so long, this time?

Lordy, but those devils are getting close. You knock down one, and there's two more taking his place. This gun gets much hotter, it's going to blow up in my face. God-almighty—they're not going to cut and run, not this time. They're coming right on in. Those troopers on the bank are holding their ground, though, even with the Sioux right on top of them. Guts—that's real guts.

Have a look at those bluecoats, you rebels who want another war. Are they the kind of men you want to murder? Sioux all around them now, shooting and yelling, with sunlight glinting from the blades in club-heads. Takes a real man to stand up to that kind of fighting. Being bullet-hit is bad enough to think about, but there's something about a sharp blade ripping in that makes a man sick, just the thought of it.

Why did they hold off with the Gatling gun so long this time? Too late for it now, maybe. Too late ....

When the overheated rifle burst its muzzle, the explosion jolted Branch McCabe's hands with a tingling numbness. A bullet ricocheted from the railing close by, screaming past his face. He rolled over and over on the deck, then lunged to his feet and went running to the stairs. He plunged down them to the main deck. At one side he saw a trooper crouching over his carbine, blinded by blood streaming down his face from a long gash across his forehead.

McCabe leaped to the man, and took the carbine from him. "I can use this better than you, friend."

The man was pawing at his eyes, shouting. "Where are they, where are they?"

McCabe ran across the deck to the railing. He saw several warriors break through the thin line of troopers along the bank and come splashing into the shallows of the river on racing ponies, making for the packet. He fired at one painted face and missed; he fired again, and the warrior pitched headlong off the pony into the water.

The carbine snapped empty; he reversed it in his big hands, gripping the barrel. A Sioux came close, pony lunging through the shallows in great bucking leaps. McCabe swung the rifle, hard, and the warrior tumbled, his mouth open in a yell that McCabe never heard.

The others came slewing in, two, three, four of them. McCabe dropped the nearest one with a hard clubbing blow, and felt the hot wind of a gunshot close against his face. He twisted around, hurling the rifle at the painted face of the Indian. The fellow ducked and came erect again, swinging up the pistol in his hand. A gunshot bellowed at McCabe's side, smashing again and again, so close that the concussions deafened his ears with their thunder. The Sioux crumpled, and the one with him yanked his pony around in frantic retreat.

It was Sam Carthage beside him, Sam and a leather-faced Yankee trooper. McCabe yelled at them. "What happened to that Gatling?" But he couldn't hear his own voice.

Sam Carthage said something, shouting. But he couldn't hear that, either. He pivoted away from them, running hard for the bow of the boat, running past men who were dead and men who sat empty-eyed on the deck, clutching the blood of torn wounds.

Then he heard a short hard burst from the Gatling gun, and he saw the man crouching behind it. Lee Malvern. The die-hard rebel, Lee Malvern.

The troopers on the bank, those of them who were left, heard that harsh rattling burst and understood the meaning of it. They dropped to the ground. The Gatling hammered into full voice then, stuttering its violence into the massed, milling Sioux. For one brief moment they swung their fury toward the packet. Then their attack lost all force and direction, and they scattered wildly, racing back to the hills.

Branch McCabe stood there, a great melting weakness rolling through him. The thunder was leaving his ears, now that the guns had stopped going off. The sudden silence was almost as bad as the head-splitting roar of battle, he thought; the silence was hard and heavy and almost hurtful.

He stood there in a kind of dull shock, barely realizing that it was all over, that the Sioux were gone. He was looking at the man who lay dead beneath the Gatling gun; it was Sergeant Geary.

There was only one explanation for the death of a Yankee sergeant who had never seen the day when he would turn away from an enemy.

The bullet that had killed him had come from behind, a carefully aimed shot that had struck him precisely between the shoulder blades.

CHAPTER TWENTY-THREE

THEY WERE THERE outside the wheelhouse, all of the packet's hard-case crew, and Elise, too. Jubal, Kennerly and Clee Yandell. Sam Carthage and Hap Burwell and Lee Malvern. These and all the others, powder-stained and grimy from the fighting, and filled with a residue of anger standing hard and strong in their eyes as they watched Branch McCabe in sober concentration.

This, McCabe knew, was the end of all waiting. These were the proud ones, the undefeated ones who had fought a futile war and had come up a long river to ignite the flames of another. Unconquered and unbowed, these men were, and if they had been kinked by old prejudices and biased traditions, McCabe could not find it in himself to pass harsh judgment on them. In his book, only those who were too hidebound and intolerantly blind to recognize and correct their mistakes were to be condemned.

Travis Hooker was there, and Logart and Lou Savaine. The malevolence of these three could be felt in the bones, and tasted in the mouth, like gall. Hooker was watching Lee Malvern, hating him with his smoldering, unblinking stare.

"You just had to cut loose with that Gatling gun," he said, and cursed Lee Malvern in a flat and savage flare of temper. "Another couple of minutes, and the Sioux could have hacked down every blue-belly on that bank. But you, damn you, just had to cut in with that Gatling!"

Angry resentment ruddied Lee Malvern's face, and he spoke out strongly against the rawhiding Hooker was giving him. "That Yankee sergeant was dead, wasn't he?"

"I know he was dead, by God!"

"He caught one in the back, poor devil."

"Right between the shoulder blades," Hooker said. "I know where he was hit, by God! Maybe you feel like crying over the bastard."

Lee Malvern stood very still, all expression withdrawing from his face. "Some one had to take his place," he said stubbornly.

"Now ain't you the big hero, though!"

"I only did what I figured had to be done."

"You yanked a bunch of bluecoats out of the fire, that's what you did," Hooker flared back at him. "So what if the Sioux had busted through and got to the boat? We could have forted our- selves up here while they had their fun with the Yankees down below. And when they came after us, we could have held them off at the stairs long enough for me to get some things across to their chiefs. I knew what I was doing. I haven't let it out of mind once what we came up this river to do. But you had to cut loose with that goddamn Gatling!"

"About that Yankee gunner," McCabe said, and saw Travis Hooker pivot sharply around. "You're the one who put that bullet in his back, are you?"

It was there to be seen in the man's flat stare, plain and with- out pretense. It was not the first time he had used such a mark for his guns. He had learned from one of the best, from Quantrill. And in his dark eyes there was a flashing of devils, jeering in malice and mockery.

"Easiest shot I ever made," Travis Hooker said, and laughed contemptuously.

No regrets, no remorse. A bullet in the back, and proud of it afterwards. It was a shocking thing that hit all men there on the

Belle's deck, and dug deep into them, and turned the pages of their own conscience.

Elise's whisper was barely audible. "To kill him like that! To murder him!"

The men stood silent. There was an edge to the hush that Travis Hooker did not like. A rising wariness took hold of his eyes, a keening glint of alerting temper.

Branch McCabe spoke slowly. "A bullet in a Yankee's back, or when he's facing you. You want them dead, you kill the easiest and safest way. Quantrill knew how, and it's something you men are going to have to learn."

Hooker's breathing was thin, shallow. He said nothing.

McCabe's smile was one of calloused indifference, as he knew it had to be. And as he spoke he wondered if this final test would prove the truth of the old saw about it taking poison to kill poison.

"No need for you to rawhide Malvern, though. You can still finish what you came up the river to do. We've all got guns. It'll be easy as knocking apples out of a tree. All we've got to do is go below and circulate among the Yankees. They won't suspect anything. Just get behind them, and when you get the signal jerk your guns and start shooting. One minute they're alive, next minute they're all dead. Easy, easy."

He laughed softly, frigidly. "Kind of funny, at that. All they'll ever get for helping a bunch of rebels keep their scalps from the Sioux is a sudden trip to their graves."

He heard the soft catch of Elise's breathing. He didn't look at her.

The men of the *Belle* were silent, and now he could detect an uneasiness moving into their eyes; it was the memory of Yankee troopers standing strong against the whiplash fury of four hundred Sioux hostiles. And there was more. They were looking into themselves and not liking what they saw. The shame of it was growing in their eyes.

McCabe went on with brutal bluntness. "The troopers out of our way, we'll dump all the quartermaster stores out on the bank for the Sioux to get. Then we'll head down-river. Turley and McKinn are running short of supplies by now. Once they fire their last shot, every warrior in the hills will come down on them. Gentlemen, you wanted your regiment of dead Yankees, and there you have it."

He looked at Kennerly and Malvern, at Clee Yandell and Carthage and Jubal. "That sound all right to you?"

Lee Malvern opened his mouth. Nothing came. All three looked away.

"Those wounded men we've got on board might be a problem, though," McCabe said. "Question is, do we shoot them, or do we just heave them into the river? It's up to you boys to say."

And now he could see the utter sickness of shame and disgust standing in their eyes.

Elise was crying out to him. "No... please, Branch!"

He looked at her, and now she was vocalizing her sobbing as a small child will. "I can't, Branch. I just can't go through with it. I've tried to be like you, like you would have wanted me to be. I've tried, tried to help you. But not this... not this, Branch!"

He stared at her intently. Then all at once he realized how completely wrong he had been about her. It was like a great door opening within him, so that for the first time he could see all the good and real things this girl had kept hidden from him.

Yet it was not done, not yet. He turned and looked at the crew, at the roustabouts.

"It'll be quick and easy," he told them. "Those you don't shoot, you can knife. This new war you came up here to start will be fought Quantrill-style. How about it, boys?"

It was Clee Yandell who spoke out for them all. "No, by God!"

A sudden knowing swept into Travis Hooker's eyes, an understanding that burst through him in a wild and hating rage to kill. His hand stabbed under his coat, to the derringer.

McCabe threw himself at the man, hearing Elise's thin cry of fear, and knowing full well that the distance was much too great. He saw the wicked glitter of the derringer as it swept up at him, and beyond it the feral promise that was in Hooker's eyes.

Only a man of Jubal's size could have done it. The Negro's long arm stabbed up and forward; his huge hand clamped around Hooker's fist, completely enclosing the small weapon so that its blast came as a soft, muffled concussion.

Jubal's hand showed a sudden torn redness, but even then he did not release his grip. He forced Hooker's arm higher, and held it locked there until the second shot tore it free.

Then McCabe was close enough. He felt the stinging pain of the derringer clubbing his face as he drove his fist home. The impact of his blow slammed Hooker back against the wall of the wheelhouse, and he saw the man's boot kicking viciously at his groin as he closed in again. He twisted aside, driving his blows to the face and body, hitting the man again and again until all resistance collapsed and was gone.

He swung around, remembering Logart and the murderous efficiency of Lou Savaine's knife. But there was no danger for him in those men, not now. Lou Savaine was down, his arm twisted to a grotesque angle across Logart's slack body.

And the men of the *Belle* stood around, smoke-stained and grimy from battle, with Clee Yandell grinning in a slow and thoughtful way.

"A funny thing," Yandell said. "This is the first time since we pulled out of Natchez that I've felt clean."

The fireboxes had been fed, and a good head of steam built up in the boilers. Clee Yandell rammed his levers home, and the bucket planks of the *Southern Belle* commenced turning, taking hold of the water.

Branch McCabe eased the bow around until it was once again pointed toward the north, toward the Yellowstone. He

raised his gaze. Yonder were the tall hills and broad valleys where men from the South would someday make homes for themselves, with men from the North for neighbors. It was a good thought. It sat warm and easy in his mind.

When the currents of the river were free and deep, he looked around at Elise. She was seated on the bench, watching him, and beneath the surface serenity of her eyes there was a hint of bold promise that sent a man's fancies surging warmly through him.

She was a vixen, for a fact, this amazingly beautiful girl. A little boldness and the proper amount of shyness mixed together in a way that brought out the bobcat that was in a man, making him feel bigger and stronger than a mountain.

She stood up, and said, "You could get someone else to take over the wheel for a while, you know."

"I reckon."

She kept her eyes on him, waiting. "Well, Branch?"

He laughed softly.

From down on the main deck, Jubal's full rich voice rose in an old familiar bayou song.